MAX'S MYSTERY TRAVELS

MYSTERY
AT THE
WHITE HOUSE:
A President is Missing!

Illustrated by Kari Moe

OTHER BOOKS IN THIS SERIES

Mystery at the Statue of Liberty:
The Unwanted Ghooost!

Mystery at the Baseball Hall of Fame:
Who Stole Babe's Bat?

ISBN: 1-888575-04-2
Library of Congress Catalog Card Number: 97-92932

MAX's Publications
23015 Del Lago Drive, D2-172
Laguna Hills, California 92653
1-800-4-MAX-008
www.maxbooks.com

Printed in the United States of America

MORE MAX BOOKS
Log on to the Internet to see my books!

Mate, I write mystery books *and* travel activity books. To learn about my books, check them out at **www.maxbooks.com**. For hours of awesome fun, check out my other Web site at **www.maxvikfunpage.com**.

Your friend,

MAX

THANK YOU!

The authors would like to thank the White House for allowing the public to tour the beautiful and historic home of the President of the United States.

A recent tour of the White House inspired the authors to write this book.

Nancy Ann Van Wie and MAX
Authors

CONTENTS

Chapter 1

The Mysterious Midnight Call

I will never forget that night. Instead of being sound asleep, like Birdie, Wally, Sydney, and Mel, I was wide awake, working on my latest mystery novel.

Just as I began to write the last chapter, the phone rang. I glanced at the clock. Midnight! Who was calling me at this hour?

In a hushed voice, hoping not to disturb the other members of my

1

household, I said, "Good evening, this is MAX."

"Good evening? It's afternoon in Washington, D.C." The caller laughed.

I recognized the voice. It was my friend, the President of the United States.

"Good day, Mate. Oops! I mean, Mr. President."

"MAX, my friend," the President replied, "I'm sorry to call you so late. I realize it's after midnight in Australia. I hope I didn't wake you?"

I wanted to say, *Me? No way! I'm wide awake, writing an awesome mystery. Wait 'till you read it, Mate.*

But something told me the President of the United States was not calling to learn about my latest mystery novel. So I answered, "No, Mr. President, you didn't wake me."

"Good!" he exclaimed. Then the President whispered, "MAX, something *very* mysterious has happened at the White House. A famous painting is missing."

"Someone stole a painting from the White House?" I asked in disbelief. "Which one is missing?"

"MAX, I can't give you too much information over the phone. But I can tell you it's *our* favorite portrait."

As soon as the President said *our*

favorite portrait, I knew exactly which painting was missing.

"Mr. President, have you contacted the White House Secret Service and the FBI?"

"No, MAX. You're the first person I've told."

"Why is that?" I asked.

The President paused, then said, "MAX, I want to hire your detective agency. Will you and your private investigators come to the White House to solve this mystery?"

"Absolutely!" I shouted.

"Good," the President said. "How soon can you leave?"

I thought for a moment. *Hmm, I need to wake up Birdie, Wally, Mel, and Sydney. That won't be easy. Then I'll pack and fuel up the jet.*

"Mr. President," I replied, "MAX's Mystery Jet will be in the air in two hours."

"Great! Oh, MAX ... "

"Yes, Mr. President."

"I'm sure glad we're friends."

"Me, too," I said, smiling. "Good-bye, Mr. President."

"Good-bye, MAX."

I hung up the phone, thinking about our friendship. It started two years ago, when the President called to tell me how much he enjoyed reading my mystery novels. I thanked him, and then the President said, "MAX, you have a brilliant mind for solving crimes. I think you should start an international detective agency."

I should? What a crazy idea, I thought. Sure, I knew how to solve make-believe mysteries. But could I solve *real* mysteries?

The President convinced me that I could, so I hired Birdie, Wally, Mel, and Sydney, the world's four brightest P.I.s (private investigators). And with their help, I opened MAX's Mystery Agency.

Now, only two years later, the President of the United States was calling *my* detective agency to solve a White House mystery!

I glanced at my watch. Time was quickly passing. I needed to wake up my four P.I.s. But which one should I wake up first?

As I started to walk toward the bedrooms, I heard a faint noise. Was it the sound of a bird, a kangaroo, a mouse, or a squirrel?

Suddenly, at the end of the hall, a light went on. I squinted to see who was there.

Hmm, just as I suspected. It was a bird.

A sick bird!

Chapter 2

The World's Brightest P.I.s

"MAX, did I hear the phone ringing, or was I dreaming?" Birdie mumbled in a low, weak voice.

As he slowly shuffled down the hall in his bathrobe and slippers, Birdie wailed, "Oooh, I don't feel so good. It must have been the extra-large pizza with pineapple and anchovies I ate. MAX, where are my tummy pills?"

"Shhh, Birdie, you'll wake up Mel, Wally, and Sydney," I whispered.

"Your pills are in the medicine cabinet, next to the toothpaste."

Birdie moaned and groaned as he slowly walked toward the bathroom. I couldn't tell if he was really sick or just acting. With Birdie, one never knew.

I heard the medicine cabinet close, then the patter of little feet approaching.

"Feeling better?" I asked, knowing that another Academy-Award perform-ance was about to begin.

Clutching his tiny stomach, Birdie cried, "Oooh, MAX, I'm sooo sick. If I'm not better by tomorrow, call Doc Toucan."

What an actor! I told myself. *I'll fix him.*

"Birdie, you look awful. Maybe your stomach needs to come out."

Birdie glared at me.

"Yes! That's it!" I insisted. "What you need is a stomach operation. I'll call Doc Toucan immediately."

"Wait!" Birdie shouted. "What if I die on the operating table?"

"Hmm, I didn't think about that," I said.

"Well, I did!" Birdie yelled. "MAX, scratch the call to the Doc."

Birdie shuffled toward his bedroom, mumbling, "What I need is rest, not a stupid stomach operation."

"Birdie, before you go to sleep, I need to tell you something."

"MAX, I'm too sick to listen."

"But, Birdie, this is important," I explained.

Birdie ignored me. He walked into his bedroom, turned off the light, and crawled into bed. "Good night, MAX. Let's hope I don't dream again about the phone ringing."

I followed Birdie into his room. "Birdie, listen to me. You weren't dreaming. It *was* a phone call. A *very* important phone call."

Birdie's eyes opened wide. He threw back the covers, and jumped out of bed! "Really, MAX? Who called?"

"The President of the United States," I answered.

"This late at night? Whoa! You are a very important koala!" Birdie chirped, fluttering up and down. "MAX, I'm impressed."

Before I could say, "Shhh, Birdie, you'll wake up the entire household," Wally hopped in, tucking her pajama top into her pouch.

"Mates, what's all the noise about?" she asked.

"Wally, listen to this!" Birdie exclaimed. "The President of the United States called MAX tonight. Is MAX a V.I.K., or what?"

"Or what?" Wally said, scratching her pouch.

"Never mind, Wally," Birdie said impatiently. "So, MAX," Birdie continued, "tell us what the President had to say."

"Okay, Mates, this is what happened. I was working on my latest mystery novel when the phone—"

"Phew!" Birdie shouted, pinching his little beak. "I smell mouse breath."

Just then Mel appeared from under my desk with his normal late-night snack.

"Hey, guys, could you keep it down. I'm trying to eat," Mel said, munching on a piece of old, smelly Swiss cheese. "Why's everyone up so late?"

"The President of the United States just called MAX," answered Wally. "Mel, did you know MAX is a V.I.P.?"

"No, Wally!" yelled Birdie. "MAX isn't a V.I.P., he's a V.I.K. Very Important Koala! Get it?"

"I get it, and I agree," Mel said. "MAX, why did the President call you at this hour of the night?"

"Mates, now that everyone is awake, I'll start my story from the beginning. I was writing the last chapter of my—"

"MAX!" shouted Wally. "We forgot Sydney."

Birdie smiled. "Yeah, isn't it wonderful without her."

I ignored Birdie's remark.

"Wally, thank you for reminding us. I'm glad one member of my detective agency remembered Sydney. Now, who's going to wake her up? Hmm, I don't see a show of hands. Birdie, how about you?"

"Me? Wake up roaring-snoring Sydney? No way!" Birdie said.

"Wally?" I continued.

"MAX, I'd rather hop to New Zealand."

"Mel," I said, "surely you're not afraid of a frail, feminine, friendly squirrel?"

"Yes, I am!" he shouted.

"Okay, okay. I admit that Sydney can be a little difficult when she wakes up."

"*A little difficult?*" everyone said.

14

"Listen, I have an idea," I said. "Let's draw straws to see who wakes up Sydney."

"No need to, MAX. Here she comes now," Birdie, Wally, and Mel said, laughing hysterically.

Oh, no! Sydney was weaving back and forth, bumping into chairs, lamps, and everything else that got in her way.

"Sydney!" I shouted. "Your sleeping blinders. You forgot to remove them."

15

"Ouch!" Mel cried as Sydney accidentally stepped on his tail.

"Who's that? Is that you, you little rodent?" Sydney snapped, before bumping into Wally.

"Hey, watch where you're going," hollered Wally.

Sydney had broken furniture, stepped on Mel's tail, bumped into Wally, and now was headed straight toward Birdie.

"Uh-oh. I'm out of here," Birdie said, flapping his wings. "Sure glad I can fly."

"MAX, where are you?" shouted Sydney. "Help me get these blasted beauty blinders off. No reason to wear them. It's impossible to get a good night's sleep in this house."

"Sydney, I'm right here," I told her.

I knew Sydney's roar was nothing to fear. Underneath that beautiful red coat of fur was a woman with a heart of gold.

Sydney adored Birdie, Mel, and Wally, although she would never admit it. And like her three friends, who secretly adored her, she was one of the world's brightest P.I.s.

As I helped Sydney take off her sleeping blinders, she asked, "Now, MAX, what's so important that it couldn't wait until I had my beauty rest?"

"Everyone, please be seated," I said.

My four P.I.s scurried for chairs, while I handed out pencils and MAX's Mystery Pads.

Once everyone was comfortable, Sydney in her favorite recliner, Mel in Wally's pouch, and Birdie by my side, I took a deep breath, and said, "Mates, the President of the United States has called upon *us* to solve a White House mystery."

Eight eyeballs stared at me.

"Really? What's the mystery?" they asked.

I thought for a moment, then said, "A President is missing."

Chapter 3

Just the Facts, MAX

My P.I.s gasped! "A missing President?" they said.

"MAX, did the President tell you *which* President is missing?" asked Mel.

"Well, not exactly," I answered.

"What?" Sydney shouted. "MAX, let me get this straight. A President is missing, you know which one, but the President didn't tell you."

"That's correct," I answered.

Four mouths dropped open wide.

"Wow! No wonder you're the world's most famous detective," Wally said. "You're good."

Birdie, Mel, and Sydney nodded in agreement.

"I'm good, but not that good," I said, laughing. "I had some help from the President. He gave me a clue."

"What clue was that?" Wally asked, ready to write the answer in her MAX's Mystery Pad.

"The President said *our* favorite portrait is missing," I replied.

"That's it?" Mel said. "From that *one* clue you knew which President was missing?"

I nodded and grinned.

Sydney frowned. "MAX, stop acting so mysterious and give us more information."

"Yeah, MAX, we want the facts," Birdie said. "Just the facts."

"All right, Mates," I replied.

I walked to my flip chart and wrote:

GEORGE WASHINGTON
DOLLEY MADISON
THE PRESIDENT'S TOUR

"MAX, what does this have to do with the President's clue?" Birdie wanted to know.

"Maybe it's some kind of secret code," Wally replied, glancing at her crime-solving buddies.

"Patience, my dear detectives, patience," I said, pointing to the first name on the flip chart.

"Now we all know that George Washington was the first President of the United States. Right?"

"Right!" everyone shouted.

"But was George Washington the first President to live in the White House?"

"Of course he was," Birdie answered.

"No, Bird Brain, he wasn't," Sydney said. "In 1800, when the White House was ready for the first President to move in, George was no longer living. He died in 1799."

Mel, stroking his whiskers, said, "MAX, I'm confused. If George Washington *wasn't* the first President to live in the White House, then who was?"

Before I could answer, Wally said, "Everyone knows that John Adams, the second President of the United States, was the *first* President to live in the White House."

"Very good, Wally," I replied. "Now, does everyone know that in 1800 when President John Adams moved into the White House he took George Washington with him?"

"Huh?" My four P.I.s said, staring at one another.

"MAX, how is that possible?" Mel asked. "You told us George Washington died in 1799."

"You're right," I agreed. "Mates, let me explain. Two years before George

Washington died, Gilbert Stuart, a famous painter, painted a portrait of George Washington. In 1800 when President Adams moved into the White House, he brought George's portrait with him."

"Ohhh, now I understand," Wally said. "It was George Washington's portrait and *not* George Washington that moved into the White House."

Birdie rolled his eyes. "MAX, this is all very interesting, but what does George's portrait have to do with the President's clue?"

"Patience, my dear Birdie, patience," I said, pointing toward Dolley Madison's name.

"Dolley Madison! I know about her," Sydney exclaimed. "She was a First Lady."

"Yes, she was," I replied, nodding. "Dolley Madison was married to James Madison, the fourth President of the United States. While he was President, the United States went to war with England. It was the War of 1812."

"I remember reading about that war," Mel added. "British troops marched into Washington, D.C., and set fire to the White House."

"Oh, no!" Wally cried. "MAX, did George's portrait burn in the fire?"

"No, Wally, it didn't," I answered. "Dolley rescued the portrait and fled the White House before the British troops arrived."

"MAX, whatever happened to George's portrait?" asked Sydney.

"After the burned White House was rebuilt, James and Dolley Madison moved back in, and so did George's portrait."

"MAX, for the last time," Birdie insisted, "what does George's portrait have to do with the President's clue?"

"Yeah, MAX, we agree with Birdie," said Wally, Mel, and Sydney. "What does George's portrait have to do with the President's clue?"

"Everything," I answered, smiling. "Mates, do you remember last year when the President invited me to dine with him at the White House?"

"Do we ever!" they shouted.

"Well, after that private dinner, the President gave me a personal tour of the White House. As we strolled from room to room, he showed me several portraits and told me the history of the White House."

"MAX, did you see George's portrait?" Sydney asked with a grin.

"Indeed I did! And when the tour was over, I told the President that George's portrait was my favorite."

"Wow!" Mel exclaimed. "What did the President say?"

"He said, 'MAX, it's my favorite portrait, too.'"

"Uh-oh, I think I know who's missing," Birdie mumbled.

Mel, Wally, and Sydney nodded.

"So, Mates, when the President called tonight and said *our* favorite portrait is missing, I immediately knew he meant—"

"George Washington!" my P.I.s shouted.

"Right you are, my four sly sleuths. Now, Mates, what do you think? Can we find George's portrait and solve the case of the missing President?"

"Yesss!" they shouted, jumping up and down.

"All right, troops, start packing," I instructed. "We're off to meet the President of the United States!"

Chapter 4

D.C., Here We Come

"MAX, while you're packing," said Birdie, "I'll fuel up the jet and make sure there's plenty of food aboard."

"Thanks, you're a great copilot," I told Birdie as he flew out the door.

"Hmm, what should I pack first?" I whispered aloud. "Let's see, I need to take my walkie-talkie, laptop computer, fax machine, cellular phone, beeper ... "

"And your Mystery Magnifying Glass," Mel added.

"Right you are, Mel. Thanks for reminding me."

"MAX, don't worry about a thing," said Mel. "Wally and I will pack everything for you."

"Thanks, guys, but where will you find a suitcase big enough?"

"Right here, MAX," replied Wally, patting her protruding pouch.

I laughed. "Great idea. Now all I have to do is get dressed."

"MAX, don't forget to wear your stars-and-stripes tie," Sydney yelled, running down the hall with her suitcase bulging. "And hurry up, we're late."

Sydney was right. It was late. It was time to board MAX's Mystery Jet for our 20-hour flight from Australia to Washington, D.C.

"Bye, MAX," my P.I.s said as they raced out the front door.

"Hey, wait for me!" I shouted.

I changed my clothes, and out the door I ran!

28

One hour later, high in the sky, MAX's Mystery Jet was headed for the White House.

In the cockpit, Birdie and I were at the controls. In the main cabin, Mel and Wally played their favorite card game, Go Fish, while Sydney, wearing her beauty blinders, slept and snored.

It was smooth flying all the way to California, where we landed at the Los Angeles International Airport to refuel and relax.

While enjoying a hot meal in the main cabin, Wally asked, "MAX, how can we find the missing portrait, if we don't know what it looks like?"

"Excellent question!" Birdie remarked. The rest of us agreed.

"Wally, thank you for reminding me," I said, rising from my seat. "Mates, I'll be right back."

I walked to the cockpit where my backpack was stored. I looked inside. Yes! There it was.

When I returned to the main cabin, Mel said, "MAX, what's that you're holding?"

"It's a book titled *An Awesome Tour of the White House*," I answered. "This book tells the history of the White House as it guides you through each room."

"MAX, is there a picture of George's portrait in that book?" Birdie asked.

Before I had a chance to answer, Sydney said, "MAX, if George is in that book, I want to see him right now."

"Okay, okay, I confess. There is a picture of George's portrait in this book."

"Hurray!" everyone shouted.

I passed the book among my four P.I.s and instructed them to study the picture *very* carefully.

When Birdie, Mel, and Sydney finished, it was Wally's turn.

"MAX, in which room did this portrait hang?" Wally asked as she closely examined the picture.

"In the East Room, the largest room in the White House," I explained. "It's so large that when First Lady Abigail Adams moved into the White House in 1800, she used to hang her laundry in the unfinished East Room."

"Wow! That's large!" Mel shouted.

Birdie agreed. "MAX, how many rooms are there in the White House?"

"The White House has over 130 rooms," I replied. "There are 34 bathrooms, two kitchens, a small movie theater, a press room, a florist shop, and much more."

"This is *so* exciting!" Sydney gushed. "I can't wait until we arrive."

Just then one of the airport mechanics entered the plane and said, "MAX, your jet is fueled up and ready for takeoff. You should be arriving in Washington, D.C. in six hours."

"Yikes!" Sydney yelled as she quickly put on her sleeping blinders. "In just six hours I have to be beautiful for the

President of the United States. MAX, wake me when we arrive in D.C., and not a second before. I need all the beauty rest I can get."

"That's for sure," Birdie mumbled under his breath.

Uh-oh, here we go, I thought.

I silently counted to ten, waiting for Sydney to explode. But luckily she hadn't heard Birdie's comment. Instead, she had fallen asleep immediately and was snoring like a baby.

I closed my eyes and smiled.

D.C., here we come!

Chapter 5

A White House Surprise

At exactly 10:22 P.M., MAX's Mystery Jet touched down at the Washington International Airport. Upon arrival, I saw a familiar automobile, the White House limousine.

"Good evening, MAX, it's nice to see you again," the limousine driver said.

"Jason, my pal," I replied, beaming, "it's good to see you, too. I'd like you to meet my friends—Birdie, Wally, Mel, and Sydney."

Jason bowed and said, "Pleased to meet you. Any friend of MAX's is a friend of mine. Is this your first trip to D.C.?"

"Yes!" my four P.I.s shouted.

"Business or pleasure?" he asked.

Oh, no! I forgot to tell my P.I.s that no one was to know of our secret mission. Before they had a chance to answer, I said, "Pleasure. My friends are eager to tour the nation's capital, and meet the President."

Jason smiled. "Well then, let me be the first to give your friends a tour of the nation's capital. Hop in!"

As we traveled up, down, and around the streets of D.C., Jason pointed out a few of the city's most famous attractions.

"Over there, on the left," he said, is the Jefferson Memorial. Thomas Jefferson, the third President of the United States, wrote the Declaration of Independence."

"Mates," I added, "the Declaration of Independence gave the United States its freedom from England. It was signed on July 4, 1776."

"Very good, MAX. I'm impressed," Jason said. "Now, if everyone will look straight ahead, you'll see the Lincoln Memorial. It was built in honor of President Abraham Lincoln."

"Jason, what's that very tall, thin building I see in the far distance?" Birdie asked.

"That building is the tallest in D.C., and one of the tallest in the world," Jason answered. "It's the Washington Monument. It's a tribute to the first President of the United States, George—"

"Washington!" everyone shouted, laughing.

Jason continued to entertain and amaze us with his historic tour of Washington, D.C. After he pointed out the Supreme Court Building and the

U.S. Capitol, he said, "My friends, this is it! Welcome to the White House. The home of the President of the United States."

My P.I.s gasped!

I glanced toward Sydney. She had mischief in her eyes.

Before I had a chance to remind my P.I.s of their manners, Sydney flung open the car door, jumped out, and started racing toward the White House.

"Last one to the White House is a rotten egg," she yelled.

"Hey, wait for me!" Mel squealed.

"Me, too!" Birdie added.

"MAX, hurry up," Wally said, hopping past me.

When I caught up with my P.I.s, they were standing on the White House steps. I glared at them. They knew they were in trouble. Big trouble!

I was just about to scold them when the front door suddenly opened.

"Good evening, MAX, we've been

expecting you," a tall, slender gentleman said. "My name's Edward. I'm a Secret Service officer. I will be escorting you and your friends to the Oval Office. Please follow me."

"Psst, MAX. I'm getting nervous," Birdie said. "My stomach feels funny. Did you pack my tummy pills?"

"Shhhh!" I whispered. "No, Birdie, I didn't pack your pills. But there's no need to be nervous. The President is my friend. Now get in line, and keep quiet."

My P.I.s and I marched toward the Oval Office in a single file. No one said a word. Then, without warning, someone shouted, "STOP!"

It was Edward.

"What's wrong?" I asked.

"MAX, I almost forgot. The President told me to take you to the East Room first."

The East Room? What for? I wondered.

"MAX, the President wants you and your friends to see George Washington's portrait," Edward explained.

My P.I.s looked shocked! They stared at me, but I said nothing.

"This way," Edward told us.

He led us past the White House Library, up the stairs, and then he turned to the right. We were now in the White House's largest room.

"Welcome to the East Room," Edward said, pointing toward a huge painting. "Here's where the famous portrait of George Washington hangs."

No way! I told myself. But there it was. I tried to examine the portrait as carefully as I could, in as little time as I had.

It appeared to be the original painting by Gilbert Stuart. Or was it? I scratched my left ear as I thought about this mystery.

"Please follow me," Edward said. "The President is waiting."

Just then we heard a loud *Thud!*

"Wally, are you all right?" I asked.

"Yes, MAX. I just tripped on my shoelace. Go ahead. I'll meet you at the end of the hall."

"Edward, is that okay?" I asked.

40

"Yes, but make it fast," he replied. "The President is waiting."

A few minutes later Wally joined us, and we continued to follow Edward toward the Oval Office.

When we arrived, the President was sitting at his desk, reading.

"Excuse me, Mr. President," said Edward. "MAX and his friends are here to see you."

The President quickly looked up, then shouted ...

Chapter 6

Operation Trip

"MAX! My pal! My buddy! It's so good to see you."

"You, too, Mr. President," I said as we hugged each other. "Mr. President, I would like you to meet—"

"Wait!" the President said. "I know, you want me to meet the world's brightest private investigators. Am I right?"

"Indeed you are," I answered. "Sydney, Birdie, Wally, and Mel, it's an honor and a privilege to introduce you to my friend, the President of the United States."

"Good evening, Mr. President," my P.I.s said as they took turns shaking his hand.

"Good evening," the President said. "Please sit down. You must be exhausted after your long flight."

Once everyone was seated, I noticed how tired the President looked.

"Mr. President, how are you feeling? You look rather tired, if you don't mind my saying so."

"MAX, ever since I discovered George Washington's portrait was missing, I haven't slept a wink."

The President glanced at my P.I.s, and then back at me. "I realize everyone is totally confused," he said, "but let me explain. The portrait of George Washington you saw in the East Room is *not* the original painting by Gilbert Stuart. The portrait you saw is a fake."

"Yes, I know," I replied.

"What?" the President said. "MAX, how could you possibly know the portrait was a fake? You weren't in the East Room for more than a minute. Or were you?"

"No, Mr. President, I wasn't. But Wally was."

"Wally?" the President said.

"Mr. President, let me explain."

"Please do, MAX. I am totally confused."

"Mr. President, when I entered the East Room tonight and saw George Washington's portrait, I suspected it was a fake."

"You did? Why is that?" he asked.

"Mr. President, if the portrait had been found, you would have called me with the good news. Am I right?"

The President grinned.

"But since you didn't call me, I suspected that the portrait hanging in the East Room was *not* the original.

With so little time to examine it, I had to think fast. That's when I gave the secret code for *Operation Trip*."

The President's eyes opened wide. *"Operation Trip?* Wow!" he shouted. "MAX, this is more exciting than reading a Sherlock Holmes mystery. Don't stop now."

"Mr. President, I think Wally should continue from this point."

"Whatever you say, MAX," the President replied. "Wally, please continue."

"Well, Mr. President, it's like this," Wally said. "When we entered the East Room and saw George's portrait, everyone was shocked! Everyone but MAX, and that made me suspicious. So I watched MAX very closely to see if anything would happen. And sure enough, it happened."

"Wally, what happened?"

"MAX scratched his left ear," Wally answered.

"His left ear?" the President said, somewhat puzzled.

"Yeah," Wally replied. "When MAX scratches his left ear that's the secret code for *Operation Trip*."

"Wally, what exactly is *Operation Trip*?"

"Oh, that's when I trip, or *pretend* to trip," Wally said proudly. "It fakes people out, every time."

The President laughed. "I'm sure it does, Wally. Please continue."

"Well, Mr. President, as soon as MAX scratched his left ear, I tripped and told everyone to go ahead; I'd meet them later. Then, right on cue, MAX asked Edward if that would be okay."

"Very clever!" the President exclaimed. "What happened next?"

"I dug into my pouch for MAX's high-powered magnifying glass. Then I examined the portrait, from head to toe. As soon as I reached the bottom, I knew the portrait was a fake!"

The President looked stunned. "Wally, how did you know that George's portrait was a fake?"

"Oh, that was easy!" Wally replied. "There was one buckle, instead of two, on George's shoes."

"Brilliant! Absolutely brilliant!" the President exclaimed. "But, Wally, how were you able to tell this to MAX without anyone hearing you?"

"Oh, I didn't tell him, I wrote it," Wally explained. "After we arrived at the Oval Office, I handed him his MAX's Mystery Pad. When MAX opened it, he read the answer."

The President sat at his desk, shaking his head. He couldn't believe his ears. He was truly amazed.

I smiled at Wally. I was so proud of her. Just as I was about to give her a high-five, there was a knock at the door. It was Edward, the Secret Service officer.

"Mr. President, your Secretary of

State needs to talk with you immediately."

"Thank you, Edward," the President replied.

"MAX, let's continue this conversation tomorrow morning. Edward will show you to your rooms." Then the President winked and said, "Good night, Mates."

We exited the Oval Office and followed Edward upstairs to the White House sleeping quarters.

Sydney had her own room. Thank goodness! She was staying in the Queens' Bedroom. This room, decorated in several shades of pink, is named for its many royal guests. In the past, queens from countries such as the Netherlands, Greece, and Great Britain have slept in this room. But tonight, the queen of the snorers, Queen Sydney, was its guest of honor.

Wally, Mel, Birdie, and I shared the Lincoln Bedroom. This a very historic room. It's where President Abraham Lincoln signed a famous document that declared freedom for all slaves in the Confederate states during the Civil War.

The Lincoln Bedroom is famous for another reason, too: the *ghost* of Abraham Lincoln!

Over the years, some people have said they've seen Lincoln's ghost in this room.

But I didn't tell that to Birdie, Wally, or Mel. After all, there's no such thing as a ghost.

Or is there?

Chapter 7

A Haunted White House?

By the time I had unpacked, put my pajamas on, brushed my teeth, and crawled into bed, it was 1 A.M.

I glanced around the Lincoln Bedroom. My roommates were sound asleep. Birdie was beside me, snoring softly, and Wally was at the foot of the bed, with Mel snuggled in her pouch.

I turned off the light, and fell asleep the moment my head hit the pillow. I slept like a baby until I heard …

"MAX! MAX, wake up!"

"What? Who said that?" I asked, glancing around the room.

"MAX, it's me," Birdie whispered.

"Birdie, what's wrong?"

"MAX, I saw something. Something *verrry* strange."

"Birdie, I told you to stop eating pizza with pineapple and anchovies before you go to bed. It makes you have weird dreams."

"MAX, this was *no* weird dream. I know I saw something. I saw a ghost! Really, I did!

"Birdie, there's no such thing as a ghost. Now go back to sleep."

"MAX, that's what I thought until I saw him."

Saw him? I said to myself.

"MAX, are you listening to me?" Birdie asked.

"Well, if he isn't, I am," Wally said, rubbing her sleepy eyes. "Now what's all this talk about a ghost?"

"Wally, I saw a ghost!"

"Really? What did it look like?"

"Well, at first, it looked like a huge ball of white cotton candy floating in the air. But then, when it floated toward me, I realized it was a ghost. The ghost of Abraham Lincoln!"

Wally's eyeballs almost popped out. "Wow!" she exclaimed. "Did Abe say anything?"

"Yes," Birdie replied. "Abe told me to *'Find the southpaw.'*"

"Find the southpaw?" said Wally. "MAX, what's a southpaw?"

"The word southpaw is slang for a left-handed person," I answered.

"MAX, isn't the President a southpaw?" Birdie asked.

I thought for a moment, then said, "Yes, Birdie, you're right. The President is left-handed."

Wally looked confused. "MAX, do you think Abe was warning us about the President?"

"No, Wally, I don't think —"

"MAX!" whispered Birdie. "Look! Under the doorway, there's a shadow. Someone's out there."

I quickly turned off the light. "Pretend you're asleep," I said.

"MAX, someone's opening the door.

I'm scared," Birdie cried.

My heart began to pound faster and faster. Who or what was entering our room at two o'clock in the morning? Was Birdie right? Had he seen the ghost of Abraham Lincoln?

The door slowly closed as a mysterious figure softly tiptoed toward the bed.

Birdie's little body started to shake. Even Wally, who holds a black belt in karate, looked scared.

As the mysterious figure got closer and closer, I had a strange feeling I knew who it was.

Suddenly Birdie screamed, "Phew! I smell mouse breath."

Ah-ha! Just as I had suspected. It *was* Mel.

"Mel! You scared us half to death," I scolded.

Mel laughed. "Hi, guys. Why are you awake? When I left, you were all snoring."

"Birdie saw a ghost!" said Wally.

"Really?"

"Mel, you missed all the action, as usual," Birdie said sarcastically.

"No way, Bird Brain. Wait until you hear what Whitney told me."

"Whitney? Who's Whitney?" asked Birdie.

"The White House mouse," Mel replied smugly.

Wally scratched her pouch. "The White House has a mouse?"

"Of course. Every house has a mouse," Mel answered. "Even the White House. Now do you want to hear my news, or not?"

"Mel, please continue," I said.

"Okay, here's what happened. I woke up starved, so I scampered down to the White House kitchen. While snooping for something to eat, this gorgeous white mouse, with the biggest pink eyes you've ever ... "

"Mel, get to the point," I insisted.

56

"Sorry, MAX. Now, where was I? Oh, yeah, she introduced herself as Whitney, the White House mouse. I asked her if it was exciting to live in the White House."

"What did she say?" asked Wally.

"She told me it's rather boring, except for this Thursday evening when there was lots of action in the florist shop."

"Mel, there's nothing unusual about that," I said. "The White House has a florist shop. The florist probably was working late that night."

"MAX, the florist shop was closed Thursday."

"Hmm, that's interesting," I replied. "Mel, did Whitney say anything else?"

"Yes. Whitney said she heard two men talking earlier in the night, around six o'clock. Then, at one o'clock in the morning, she heard a loud noise."

Birdie, nervously fluttering up and down, said, "MAX, do you think this has anything to do with the portrait that was stolen Thursday evening?"

"I'm not sure," I answered. "Listen, Mates, not a word of this to the President."

I turned off the light, and prayed for silence.

Soon my roommates were sound asleep, but not me. I tossed and turned. I couldn't stop thinking about everything that had happened.

Did Birdie really see Abraham Lincoln's ghost? Did a southpaw steal George's portrait? Did Whitney hear noises in the florist shop Thursday evening?

My eyes started to feel heavy. My body started to relax. Before I knew it, I was sleeping, and dreaming.

I dreamed someone was knocking at the door.

Wait! It wasn't a dream. Someone *was* knocking at the door!

Oh no! Who could it be?

58

Chapter 8

Rise and Shine, Mates

"MAX, are you awake? Let me in! Open this door, right now!"

Uh-oh! I had overslept and my roommates had, too!

I stumbled to the door and shouted, "Sydney, I'm coming."

When I opened the door, I could not believe my eyes. Sydney looked gorgeous! She was wearing a royal blue dress with a hat to match, and of course, her red high heels.

"What are you staring at?" she snapped.

"Syd, you look beautiful," I said.

"I always look beautiful," she replied. "Now get out of my way."

Sydney pushed the door open, marched past me, and stormed toward the bed. Roaring-snoring Sydney was about to explode.

60

In a booming voice she instructed, "Birdie, drag your tail feathers; Wally, hop in the shower; Mel, brush your teeth. Right now! Phew! This room smells like rotten cheese."

Uh-oh! I knew my time had come.

"And you, MAX, what's your excuse for oversleeping? The President is expecting us in thirty minutes."

"Syd, you wouldn't believe it if I told you."

"Probably not," she said. "And anyway, I don't have time to listen. I'm starved."

Sydney marched out the door, but not before she shouted, "MAX, I'll meet you in the dining hall in ten minutes. And don't be late!"

I glanced at my roommates. They were scurrying around the room faster than they had ever moved.

We all knew that Sydney was right. The President was expecting us and we couldn't be late.

Don't ask me how we did it, but nine minutes and fifty-nine seconds later, Birdie, Wally, Mel, and I walked into the dining room.

"Good morning," Sydney said, smiling. "It's so nice to see my four best friends. I've missed you."

Birdie, Wally, and Mel stared at me. I knew what they were thinking: Is this the same Sydney who stormed into our room just ten minutes earlier?

Yes, it was, but now her stomach was full.

"Sydney, have you eaten breakfast yet?" Of course I knew the answer.

"Oooh, yes," she swooned. "I highly recommend the waffles with fresh strawberries and whipped cream." Sydney winked at the White House waiter. "In fact, I think I'll have another helping."

After we were served and the White House waiters left the room, Birdie told Sydney that he had seen *and* heard the ghost of Abraham Lincoln.

"A talking ghost?" she yelled. "Rats! I missed all the fun."

"Sydney, it wasn't fun," Birdie said. "It was scary."

Sydney wasn't listening; she was deep in thought. "Birdie, I wonder why Abe didn't float over to the Queens' Bedroom and talk to me?"

Birdie smiled. "Ohhh, but he did."

"He did?" Sydney asked.

"Yes," Birdie replied. "Abe told me he tried to talk to you, but you were snoring so loudly you didn't hear him."

"Really?" Sydney said, not noticing that everyone was giggling.

"It's true, Syd," Wally replied with a straight face. "Then, when Abe realized you couldn't see him because you were wearing sleeping blinders, he floated back to our room."

"Mel, is that true?" Sydney asked.

"Don't ask Mel," said Birdie. "When Abe was visiting our room, Mel was in

63

the White House kitchen flirting with Whitney."

"Whitney? Who's Whitney?" shouted Sydney.

Uh-oh, I said to myself. *I'd better tell Sydney what really happened last night.*

"Sydney, I have something to tell you."

When I finished my story, Sydney said, "MAX, let me get this straight. Everything you told me about Abe's ghost and the White House mouse happened last night, while I was sleeping in the Queens' Bedroom."

"Yes, that's correct," I answered.

"That does it!" Sydney yelled. "MAX, forget the Queens' Bedroom. Tonight, I'm sleeping in the Lincoln Bedroom with you guys—where the action is."

Before Birdie, Wally, Mel, and I had a chance to tell Sydney there was no way she was sleeping in the Lincoln Bedroom with us, Edward entered the dining room.

"Good morning, MAX," Edward said cheerfully. "I'm here to escort you and your friends to the Oval Office. Please follow me."

Chapter 9

Just the Facts, Mr. President

When we entered the Oval Office, the President looked rested. Smiling, he said, "Good morning, Mates. I trust you all had a good night's sleep."

I wanted to say, *Mr. President, do you believe in ghosts?* But instead I just smiled and nodded, and my P.I.s did the same.

"Good! Now, MAX, let's get down to business," the President said. "I know you're eager to learn more about the missing portrait, so fire away."

I opened my MAX's Mystery Pad, glanced over my notes, then asked my first question.

"Mr. President, when did you discover George's portrait was a fake?"

"MAX, I discovered it Friday morning. The morning after the dinner-awards ceremony."

"What dinner-awards ceremony?"

"Thursday evening, in the East Room, we held a ceremony for the winners of the Fourth-Grade National Spelling Bee."

"Mr. President, who attended the ceremony?"

"Well, let's see. There were 50 fourth graders, plus parents and teachers. Oh, and of course the First Lady and I attended."

"Did you have anything good to eat?" I asked with a big smile.

"Boy, did we!" the President exclaimed. "We had pizza, garlic bread, salad, and hot fudge sundaes for dessert."

"Yum, my kind of meal," I remarked. "Mr. President, were there flowers on the tables?"

"Oh, yes, MAX. Each table had a

beautiful flower arrangement with a balloon attached that said *congratulations*." The President grinned. "That was my idea," he explained.

"Mr. President, did the White House florist make the flower arrangements?"

"No, MAX, he didn't. The White House florist is on vacation this week, so we used a company named Flowers Unlimited."

"Had you used Flowers Unlimited before?" I asked.

"Yes, lots of times. Flowers Unlimited is owned by the same company that rents tables and chairs to the White House."

"Ohhh, so the tables and chairs used for the dinner-awards ceremony were rented."

"That's correct," the President replied.

Just then there was a knock at the door. It was Edward with lemonade for everyone. While he poured the pitcher of lemonade with his left hand, I noticed that Edward was wearing his wristwatch on his right hand.

Hmm, very interesting, I thought.

I jotted down a few notes in my MAX's Mystery Pad. Then, once Edward had left the room, I asked my next question.

"Mr. President, did anything unusual happen Thursday evening?"

After a long pause he said, "MAX, something unusual *did* happen. A Flowers Unlimited employee broke a vase. I remember that because the Secret Service officer who picked up the broken vase cut his right hand."

"Do you remember what happened next?"

"Yes. The officer escorted the Flowers Unlimited employee to the White House florist shop, so he could replace the broken vase."

"Would you happen to know what time they went to the florist shop?"

The President thought for a moment. "Oh, it probably was about six o'clock because the awards dinner started at seven."

I glanced at Mel. I knew what he was thinking: maybe Whitney *had* given us a valuable clue.

"Mr. President, did you see the two men return from the florist shop?"

"Well, now that you mention it, I didn't see the Flowers Unlimited employee return, but I did see the Secret Service officer. It was Edward."

"Hmm, that's interesting," I whispered under my breath.

"Mr. President, did anything unusual happen once the ceremony ended?"

"No, MAX, I don't think so. The ceremony ended around eleven o'clock. Shortly after that, Flowers Unlimited returned for their vases, tables, and chairs. But there's nothing unusual about that."

"Mr. President, I'm confused.

Why didn't Flowers Unlimited pick up their vases, tables, and chairs Friday morning, instead of returning so late Thursday night?"

"MAX, that's easy to explain," the President said. "Friday morning I had a bill-signing ceremony in the East Room, so the room needed to be cleaned the night before."

"Oh, now I understand. It was Friday, after your bill-signing ceremony, when you discovered that George's portrait was a fake."

The President shook his head. "No, MAX, it was before the ceremony. In fact, I discovered the fake portrait at six o'clock in the morning."

"Six o'clock in the morning? Mr. President, why were you in the East Room so early?"

"MAX, each morning, before I start my day, I visit George's portrait. Viewing his portrait gives me strength and courage to lead this great nation, just as President Washington did more than 200 years ago." The President paused and wiped his eyes.

It was time to ask my final question.

"Mr. President, what did you notice about George's portrait Friday morning that convinced you it was not the original portrait?"

The President slowly answered, "One buckle, instead of two, on George's shoes."

I glanced at Wally from the corner of my eye. She was beaming.

"Thank you, Mr. President. This has been very helpful. Very helpful, indeed."

"My pleasure, MAX." The President smiled. "Now, if you'll excuse me, I have to attend a *very* important meeting."

We all laughed. The President's *very* important meeting was his Sunday golf game.

The President rose from his chair, and escorted us to the door. That's when Birdie whispered in my ear.

"Oh, Mr. President," I said. "I almost forgot. Could you do me a favor?"

"Of course, MAX. What is it?"

"Could you please find out if any of the Flowers Unlimited employees who worked Thursday evening are left-handed."

The President looked puzzled. "Sure, no problem," he said. "But, MAX, why do you want to know if someone's a southpaw like me?" The President laughed.

"Umm, umm, call it a ghostly hunch," I answered.

"A ghostly hunch?" the President mumbled.

I pretended not to hear his remark and quickly said, "Mr. President, I also need to know if any of the Secret Service officers who were on duty Thursday evening are left-handed."

"MAX!" the President shouted. "Surely you don't suspect a Secret Service officer. Do you?"

"Mr. President," I replied, "everyone who was in the East Room Thursday evening is a suspect."

The President turned white as a ghost. "Including me?" he asked.

Chapter 10

Is Edward a Southpaw?

As soon as we exited the Oval Office, my P.I.s said, "MAX, you don't think—"

"No, Mates, I don't think the President is a suspect."

"Phew," Wally said, wiping her brow. "But do you suspect a Secret Service officer?"

"Possibly," I answered.

"MAX, do you think a Flowers Unlimited employee stole the portrait?"

Mel asked.

"Possibly," I repeated.

Sydney frowned. "MAX, what's going on?"

"Yeah, MAX, what's up?" my other P.I.s wanted to know.

"Mates, I'm not exactly sure. But I have a hunch that Edward is *not* who we think he is."

"What!" everyone shouted.

"Mates, do you remember when the President said Edward was the officer who cut his right hand when he picked up the broken vase?"

"Yes," they answered, bobbing their heads up and down.

"Well, if that's true, then I think Edward is right-handed."

"MAX, why do you say that?" asked Sydney.

I paused, then said, "Sydney, let me ask you a question. "Are you right-handed or left-handed?"

"I'm right-handed," she replied.

"Sydney, if you dropped a vase, would you pick it up with your right hand or left hand?"

Sydney pretended to drop something and then pick it up. "MAX, I'd pick the vase up with my right hand," she said.

"And if you had cut that hand picking up the vase, would you have cut your right hand or left hand?" I asked.

"My right hand, of course," she answered.

"Thank you, Sydney. I rest my case."

"MAX, what does that prove?" Mel asked. "The President already told us that Edward is the officer who picked up the vase and cut his right hand. So we know he's right-handed."

"Mel, I'm not so sure about that. I don't think Edward *is* right-handed."

Birdie's mouth opened wide. "Oh, no!" he cried. "Is Edward *really* a southpaw?"

"Yes, Birdie, I believe so," I replied, nodding.

Mel stroked his whiskers and said, "MAX, what makes you think Edward is left-handed? Do you have any evidence to prove it?"

"Mel's right," Sydney agreed. "What's your evidence?"

"Mates, when Edward poured the lemonade, I noticed three things. One, he poured with his left hand. Two, he didn't have a cut on his right hand. And three, Edward was wearing his wristwatch on his right wrist, like many southpaws do."

"Hmm, sure sounds like a Southpaw to me," said Wally. "But how can we be certain?"

"I guess we'll just have to wait until the President tells us if any Secret Service officers are left-handed," Sydney answered.

I grinned. "Oh, I think we'll find out before then. In fact, I'm certain of it."

"MAX, you're up to something," said Birdie.

"You're right, I am. But first I need more evidence. And I know exactly where to find it."

"Where?" my P.I.s asked.

"At the White House florist shop," I answered. "Follow me!"

Chapter 11

A Room Full of Evidence

As soon as we entered the florist shop, I noticed something unusual. "Ah-ha!" I shouted.

"MAX, what is it?" my P.I.s asked.

"Mates, I think I have found a *very* important clue. Wally, my magnifying glass, please."

Wally reached into her pouch. "Here you go, MAX," she said, handing me my Mystery Magnifying Glass.

I closely examined the evidence.

"Yes! Just as I suspected. There are *two* sets of footprints."

"What's so unusual about that?" said Sydney. "The President told us he saw the Flowers Unlimited employee and Edward come down here together."

"That's true, Sydney. But look here," I said, pointing toward the steps.

Sydney squinted her eyes as she examined the stairs. "MAX, what are you talking about? I don't see anything."

"Here, use my high-powered magnifying glass," I suggested.

"Wow!" shouted Sydney. "There's only *one* set of footprints!"

"Hey, let me look," said Birdie, grabbing the magnifying glass.

"I'm next," Wally remarked.

"Don't forget me," Mel added.

"Mates, while you're examining the footprints, think about this question: If two people came down the stairs, why is there only *one* set of footprints going back up?"

No one said a word until Sydney replied, "Well, we know that Edward went back up."

"Maybe, maybe not," I said.

"But the President saw him," Mel insisted.

"Maybe, maybe not," I repeated.

"MAX!" cried Birdie. "Stop saying that. You're driving me crazy!"

"Me, too!" everyone else agreed.

I laughed. "Listen, Mates, maybe the President *thought* he saw Edward return from the florist shop."

Eight eyeballs stared at me. "Huh?" my P.I.s said.

"Mates, I'll explain later, but right now—"

"MAX!" shouted Birdie. "Excuse me for interrupting, but there's a mouse coming towards us. And it isn't Mel."

"It's Whitney!" Mel exclaimed.

"Hi, Mel," Whitney said softly. "I hope I'm not intruding."

"No, not at all," Mel replied. "I'd

like you to meet my friends. MAX, Birdie, Wally, and Sydney, this is Whitney, the White House mouse."

We smiled and said hello.

"Mel, I remembered something else that happened Thursday night."

Mel stared at Whitney like a lovesick mouse. "Really? What is it?"

"After I heard the loud noise, I decided to go down to the florist shop and investigate."

"Whitney, did you find anything?" I asked.

"Yes, MAX," she said, handing me a piece of paper. "I hope it's important."

I glanced at the note. "Whitney, where did you find this?"

Whitney pointed toward the florist cooler. "Over there, MAX," she said. "In front of the cooler door."

"What's a cooler?" Wally wanted to know.

"It's where fresh flowers are stored," I answered.

Just then I heard a voice upstairs. It was Edward's.

"Mates!" I whispered. "We need to get going."

While I stuffed the piece of paper in my pocket, I quickly said, "Whitney, if I need your help again, can I count on you?"

"Absolutely, MAX."

"Thanks, Whitney," I said, smiling.

I glanced toward my P.I.s. "Troops, follow me," I instructed. "*Operation Flirt and Flutter* is about to begin!"

Chapter 12

Operation Flirt and Flutter

When we reached the top of the stairs, I spotted Edward at the end of the hall.

"Sydney," I whispered, "are you ready for *Operation Flirt and Flutter?*"

"Absolutely!" she said. "Who's my victim?"

"Edward," I answered.

Sydney stared at me. "Edward? The Secret Service officer?" she asked.

"That's the one," I said. "I want

you to ask Edward for his autograph."

"His autograph?"

"Yes, his autograph," I replied. "And Syd, don't forget your mission is *Operation Flirt and Flutter.*"

Sydney was grinning from ear to ear. "Honey," she said, "get ready for the performance of your life."

"Good luck, Sydney," everyone whispered as she wiggled down the hall in her blue satin dress, matching hat, and red high heels.

I quickly motioned to Birdie, Wally, and Mel to follow me. Together we hid near a table where Edward couldn't see us, but we could see him—and Sydney. This was one performance we didn't want to miss.

"Hello, Edward," Sydney said softly, fluttering her thick, black eyelashes.

Edward rolled his eyes. I'm sure he wanted to say, *Oh, brother!* But instead, he said, "Sydney, where are MAX and the rest of your friends?"

"Oh, they'll be here shortly," Sydney answered, stroking her long, furry, red tail. "Edward, I'm so impressed you're a Secret Service officer."

"You are?" he said.

"Yes, I am," Sydney replied. "I don't know anyone whose job is more important than yours. Except for the President's."

"Boy, is she laying it on thick," said Birdie.

"Shhh, be quiet," I ordered.

Sydney stared straight into Edward's eyes and sweetly said, "May I have your autograph?"

Edward looked shocked *and* flattered. "Oh, you don't want my autograph. Do you?"

"Yes, I do!" Sydney exclaimed. "When I tell my girlfriends I met a handsome, intelligent, muscular Secret Service officer, I'll have your autograph to prove it."

"Oh, how sickening!" Birdie cried.

"Shhh! Birdie, I'm warning you," I said. "Keep your big beak shut!"

I glanced at Edward. He was blushing as he autographed Sydney's piece of paper.

After Edward finished writing, Birdie, Wally, Mel, and I walked toward him.

"Hello, Edward," I said. "Is the President back from his golf game?"

Edward looked startled. "Oh, umm, hello, MAX. Umm, I'll go check," he stammered. "I'll go right now."

When Edward was out of sight, we all started giggling.

"Well, what do you think?" asked Sydney.

"You were terrific!" Mel announced.

"Yeah, Syd, you deserve an Academy Award," Wally said, clapping her hands.

I gave Sydney a big hug. "Sydney, congratulations on a job well done. We're all very proud of you. Aren't we, Birdie?"

Birdie frowned. "So let's see Mr. Wonderful's autograph. I'm sure he didn't write anything else."

Sydney laughed. "Oh, don't be so sure of that, Bird Brain."

Birdie grabbed the note from Sydney's hand. Here's what he read.

SYDNEY,

I THINK YOU'RE ADORABLE!

YOUR SECRET ADMIRER,

EDWARD

When Birdie finished reading, he dropped the note with one hand and clutched his stomach with the other. "Oooh, I think I'm going to get sick," he moaned. "Call Doc Toucan."

Sydney glared at Birdie, while Wally, Mel, and I tried not to laugh.

Suddenly, I saw someone walking toward us. It was Edward.

"Shhh, Mates. I need to tell you something before Edward gets here."

"What is it?" they asked.

"Edward wrote Sydney's note with his left hand."

My P.I.s gasped!

"Oh, no!" cried Birdie. "That means Edward really *is* a southpaw."

Chapter 13

Is the Southpaw Guilty?

We followed Edward to the Oval Office. When my P.I.s and I entered, the President was sitting behind his desk, looking relaxed and sunburned.

"Mr. President, how was your golf game?" I asked.

"Great game, MAX!" the President exclaimed. "I shot a hole-in-one! It's my lucky day." The President grinned. "And MAX," he continued, "it's your lucky day, too."

"It is?" I said.

The President nodded. "MAX, you were right about someone being a southpaw. It's—"

"Edward!" I shouted.

The President looked surprised. "Edward? No, not Edward," he replied.

My P.I.s stared at me in disbelief.

"But, Mr. President, if Edward isn't left-handed, then who is?"

"An employee of Flowers Unlimited. His name is Jack McDiver," the President explained. "He was born in Dallas, Texas. For the past ten years, Jack has been living in Paris, France. But last week he returned to the United States and started working for Flowers Unlimited."

"Mr. President, is Jack McDiver still working for Flowers Unlimited?"

"No, MAX, he isn't. Jack McDiver's last job was Thursday evening. The night he worked in the East Room."

Hmm, I'm not surprised, I thought.

Just then the President's phone rang.

"Excuse me, MAX. I need to take this call."

While the President talked on the phone, I remembered the note Whitney found near the cooler. I pulled it from my shirt pocket and read it for the first time. I couldn't believe my eyes! As soon as I finished reading the note, I knew who had stolen George's portrait.

"Thank you for calling," I heard the President say.

I quickly stuffed the note back into my pocket.

"Well, MAX, what do you think?" the President asked. "Is Jack McDiver our man?"

"Yes, Mr. President. I think Jack McDiver stole George's portrait."

"MAX, if that's true, McDiver has probably left the country by now with George's portrait." The President reached for his phone and said, "I'm going to call the FBI right now."

"No!" I shouted. "Not yet!"

The President looked stunned. "Why not?" he asked.

"Mr. President, Jack McDiver has *not* left the country. In fact, he's in the White House."

"Really? Where?"

"I can't answer that right now, but in a few hours I'll explain everything. Please trust me."

The President nodded.

"Thank you," I said. "Now, Mr. President, I have a plan to capture Jack McDiver but I will need your help."

"Of course, MAX. Just name it."

"First, I want to make sure that no one—including the FBI and the White House Secret Service officers—learns about our conversations."

"Whatever you say, MAX."

"Second, I need you to send Edward on an errand. I don't care where he goes. Just make sure he leaves the White House for at least two hours."

The President tilted his chair back and closed his eyes. After a long pause, he sat up and shouted, "Crystal City Plaza!"

"Huh?" I mumbled.

"Crystal City Plaza," the President repeated. "That's where I'll send Edward. The First Lady wants to go shopping this evening, so I'll have Edward take her."

"Brilliant idea!" I exclaimed. "Oh, Mr. President, just one more thing."

"Yes, MAX."

"Mr. President, what is Edward's last name?"

"His last name is Smith."

"Do you know Edward's middle name?"

"No, MAX, but I can find out," he replied.

The President opened his desk drawer and took out a sheet of paper. "Here are the names of the Secret Service officers," he said, glancing down the list. "Oh, here it is. Edward's middle name is McDiver."

"McDiver?" everyone shouted.

The President looked worried.

"MAX," he said, "Edward is one of my most loyal employees. I can't believe there's any connection between Jack McDiver, Edward McDiver Smith, and George's portrait."

"Don't worry, Mr. President. I'm positive Edward didn't steal George's portrait."

"Whew! That's a relief," he said.

I quickly glanced at my watch. "Mr. President, it's time to send Edward to Crystal City Plaza."

"Okay, MAX, I'll call him now."

When my P.I.s and I walked out of the Oval Office, we noticed someone coming down the hall.

"Here comes Edward," Sydney announced.

"No," I said. "Here comes Jack."

Chapter 14

The Real Edward Is Found

"Jack? Jack who?" My P.I.s asked.

"Jack McDiver," I answered.

"MAX, do you think Jack McDiver is pretending to be Edward?" asked Birdie.

"Yes, I do."

Sydney looked shocked. "MAX, if you're right, then where's the *real* Edward?"

"In a safe, cold place," I said, smiling. "Follow me, Mates."

I led my P.I.s straight to the White

House florist shop. I opened the cooler door and there, sitting in the middle of the cooler, gagged and bound, was the missing Secret Service officer.

My P.I.s gasped! "It's Jack!" they shouted.

"No, it's Edward," I answered. "The *real* Edward."

"But he looks exactly like Jack McDiver," Sydney observed.

"That's right, he does. And he should," I said. "Jack and Edward are twins. Identical twins."

"Wow!" my P.I.s exclaimed.

Edward looked frightened and confused. While my P.I.s untied him, I introduced myself.

"Edward, my name is MAX. I'm a friend of the President's. I own an international detective agency, and these are my private investigators, Birdie, Wally, Mel, and Sydney. We're here to rescue you."

Edward smiled. "Boy, am I ever glad to meet you," he said. "MAX, did you catch my brother yet?"

"No, we haven't," I answered. "Edward, we need to know what happened Thursday evening."

"MAX, I'm not sure how much I

remember, but I'll try."

Edward took a deep breath, then started his story.

"I was on duty in the East Room when Flowers Unlimited arrived. Shortly after they started to set up the chairs, tables, and flower arrangements, I heard a loud crash. When I looked around the room, I saw a Flowers Unlimited employee standing over a broken flower vase."

"What did you do?"

"I rushed over and picked up the broken pieces."

"Is that how you cut your right hand?"

Edward nodded, rubbing his wound.

"Did you recognize the Flowers Unlimited employee?"

"No, MAX, I didn't."

Hmm, that's interesting, I thought.

"Edward, once you picked up the broken vase, what happened next?"

"The Flowers Unlimited employee asked me if he could borrow a vase from the White House florist shop."

"And what did you say?"

"I knew it would be okay, even though the florist shop was closed, so I told him to follow me." Edward paused for a moment, then said, "MAX, what happened next is a total blur."

"Why? What do you mean?"

"MAX, all I remember is feeling a thump on my head, then falling to the ground. When I woke up, I was here— in the cooler—bound, gagged, and wearing this Flowers Unlimited uniform."

"Edward, did anything happen later that night?"

"Yes, MAX. Around one o'clock the cooler door opened. A man wearing *my* Secret Service officer uniform and badge entered with a huge package."

"Is that the package?" I asked, pointing toward a large object, resting on the back wall.

"Yes, that's the one."

"Edward, did you recognize the person carrying the package?"

"MAX, I couldn't believe my eyes!" Edward exclaimed. "It was my brother, Jack."

"Did Jack say anything?"

"Yes. He apologized for hitting me over the head and holding me prisoner in this cooler."

"Ah-ha!" I shouted. "Just as I suspected from the beginning. The Flowers Unlimited employee who broke the vase, hit you over the head, dragged you into this cooler, and exchanged his uniform for yours, was your brother, Jack."

"I'm afraid so," Edward replied sadly.

"MAX, I'm confused," Wally confessed. "If the Flowers Unlimited employee was really Edward's twin brother, why didn't Edward recognize Jack when he first saw him in the East Room?"

Birdie, Mel, and Sydney stared at Wally. "Good question!" they said.

"Yes, it is a good question," I agreed. "And the answer is: Jack was wearing a disguise." I glanced at Edward. "Am I right?"

"Yes, MAX," he answered. "When I first saw Jack he was wearing a fake mustache, beard, wig, and glasses."

"Ah-ha! Just as I suspected," I said. "And if we open the black duffel bag, over in the corner, I bet we'll find those items."

I nodded to Mel. He knew what to do. Mel scampered to the bag, and investigated the contents. "MAX, it's all here!" he reported.

I thought for a moment, then asked my next question. "Edward, did Jack tell you what's wrapped in that large package?"

"Yes, MAX. He told me it was George Washington's portrait."

"Did Jack say why he was hiding George's portrait in the cooler?"

"Hmm, let me think," Edward said. "Oh, yeah, now I remember. Jack sure was mad at someone. I guess this person packed the tables, chairs, and vases in the truck, but didn't leave enough room for George's portrait. So Jack had to hide George in the cooler."

Edward paused and scratched his head. "MAX, do you have any idea what's going on?"

"Yes, Edward, I do."

"You do?" my P.I.s said.

I reached into my pocket and took out a piece of paper. "Mates, do you remember the note Whitney found in front of the cooler?"

106

My four P.I.s bobbed their heads up and down.

"Well, Mates, that note turned out to be a *very* important clue."

As my P.I.s stared at me, I read the note out loud. Here's what I read.

JACK,

I SCREWED UP! AFTER I PACKED EVERYTHING, THERE WASN'T ROOM IN THE TRUCK FOR GEORGE.

I'LL BE BACK SUNDAY EVENING. MIDNIGHT. BACK DOOR, FLORIST SHOP.

AND DON'T BE LATE!

BIG JOHN

"B-big J-john?" everyone said with trembling voices.

"M-M-MAX," Birdie stuttered, "how "big is Big J-john?"

"We'll find out soon," I answered.

"We will?" my four P.I.s said as they huddled together in fear.

Suddenly, I heard a noise upstairs.

"Shhh. We don't have much time, so listen carefully," I said. "At midnight, *Operation Rescue* goes into motion."

"Hurray!" my P.I.s cheered.

Edward looked confused. "What's *Operation Rescue*?" he asked.

"Oh, it's a great plan," Birdie said. "It catches the criminals every time."

"Yeah, but sometimes it's very dangerous," Wally added.

"And that's the way we like it," Sydney said, smiling. "The more dangerous, the better."

Edward gulped. "You do?"

"Don't worry, Edward," I assured him. "Every time we have used *Operation Rescue*, it's been very successful."

Edward sighed. "MAX, whatever it takes to capture my brother and Big John, I'm all for it."

"Thanks, Edward. Now, here's how *Operation Rescue* will work."

When I finished explaining my plan, I glanced at my watch.

"Mates! It's getting late. And we still have to meet with the President."

As my P.I.s and I quickly ran out of the cooler, Edward hollered, "Good luck, MAX, and tell the President I said hi."

Chapter 15

Operation Rescue

After I told the President about *Operation Rescue* he said, "MAX, it's a brilliant plan, but much too dangerous."

"Mr. President, I knew you were going to say that. So I have something special for you."

I glanced toward Wally and winked. Smiling, she took a tiny earphone from her pouch and handed it to the President.

The President looked confused. "MAX, why do I need this?"

"Mr. President, this state-of-the-art earphone will allow you to hear everything. Now you'll be informed, every step of the way."

The President laughed. "MAX, you think of everything."

My P.I.s nodded in agreement.

"Psst, excuse me, MAX," whispered Birdie, pointing toward the clock on the wall. "It's almost midnight. We need to get going."

Birdie was right. It was almost time for *Operation Rescue*!

I rose from my seat. "Mr. President, any questions before I leave?"

"No, MAX. I know what I have to do. I'll call the FBI, right now."

My P.I.s and I said good-bye to the President, and started on our secret mission.

We quietly walked through the long corridors of the White House, then tiptoed down the dark, creaky stairs that lead to the florist shop.

112

I aimed my flashlight on the cooler, then slowly opened its big, heavy door.

Edward jumped! "Whew, thank goodness it's you, MAX. This place is starting to give me the creeps."

"I know what you mean," I said. "It's really spooky down here."

My four P.I.s agreed.

"Edward, are you ready for *Operation Rescue*?" I asked.

"Absolutely," he answered.

"Great!" I replied. "Now, let's review our plan. Mel, when Jack enters the cooler, where will you be hiding?"

"I'll be hiding behind Edward," Mel answered.

"Very good," I said. "And Birdie, where will you be hiding?"

"MAX, I'll be up there, behind the red flower pot," Birdie said, pointing toward the highest shelf.

"Excellent!" I exclaimed. Then I glanced toward Wally and Sydney. "And where will the two of you be hiding?"

"Outdoors," they said, smiling.

"Yes! All systems go," I shouted.

"Wally, the microphone, please. It's time to get Edward wired."

I placed the microphone under his collar and said, "Edward, this is a very dangerous mission. If you want to back out, it's not too late."

"No way!" he replied. "MAX, *Operation Rescue* is a brilliant plan. I know it's going to work."

"Thank you, Edward. Now it's time to tie you up. When Jack returns tonight, we don't want him to suspect a thing."

"MAX, it's Whitney!" Wally shouted as she handed me my walkie-talkie.

I pulled up the antenna and listened to the caller say, "Whitney to MAX. Can you hear me? Whitney to MAX. Come in, please."

"Whitney, it's MAX. You're coming in loud and clear."

"MAX, you were right. Jack's on his way to the florist shop."

"Good job, Whitney," I replied. "Over and out."

115

I glanced around the room. My P.I.s and Edward looked nervous. But not me! I was brave as a bat.

"Quick! Everyone take your position," I ordered. "Jack's on his way."

Mel scampered behind Edward, Birdie flew to the highest shelf and hid behind the red flower pot, and Sydney and Wally ran outdoors.

I quickly exited the cooler, then squeezed behind a workbench near the stairs.

Suddenly, as I sat alone in the dark, I didn't feel so brave. My heart started to pound. My legs started to shake.

Calm down, MAX, I told myself. *Everything will be okay.*

I took a deep breath and tried to relax. But then I heard something.

Footsteps!

Someone was coming down the stairs.

I peeked around the workbench to see who it was. Just then a mysterious figure tiptoed past me, opened the cooler door, and walked inside.

Was it Jack McDiver? I couldn't be sure. It was too dark to tell.

I quickly turned up the volume on my earphone. At first I didn't hear any noises in the cooler.

But then I heard something.

It was a voice.

It was Jack's voice!

Chapter 16

Thump! Crack! Surrender!

"Well, Edward, I see you're still bound and gagged," Jack said, laughing.

He walked past his twin brother toward the back of the cooler, then picked up the portrait.

"Sorry I can't stay longer, but George and I have an important date," Jack explained. "We're leaving the country tonight."

Suddenly, a mysterious voice said, "Jack, don't do it."

Jack's eyes got as big as saucers. "What? Who said that?" Jack asked, glancing around the room.

"Jack, I am your conscience," the mysterious voice whispered.

"My what?" Jack said.

"I am your conscience," the voice repeated. "I know right from wrong. And stealing is wrong. What would your mother say if she could see you now?"

"My mother? What do you know about my mother?"

"Ahh, I know everything about your mother," the mysterious voice answered.

"Oh, yeah. If you're so smart, what's my mom's first name?"

"Her name is Elizabeth."

Jack looked shocked. "A lucky guess," he said. "What's my mom's middle name?"

"Her middle name is Ann."

Jack felt his heart beating faster. He thought for a moment, then said, "Okay, Mr. Smarty Conscience, you're right. My mom's middle name is Ann. But I bet you don't know her maiden name."

The mysterious voice laughed. "Oh,

Jack, that's too easy. Your mom's maiden name is Jackson. When you were born your mother named you Jackson, in honor of her family name. Jack's your nickname."

Jack couldn't believe his ears! A chill ran down his back. His palms began to sweat.

"Jack, don't steal George's portrait," the mysterious voice continued. "Return it to the President."

"Yeah, right! In your dreams," Jack said. "I'll just walk into the Oval Office and say, 'Mr. President, please forgive me. I'm the one who stole your favorite portrait from the East Room.'"

"Jack, trust me," the voice said. "The President is a really cool guy. He'll understand."

"Well, maybe so," Jack replied, "but it's too late now. Big John is waiting for me."

Jack held the portrait firmly and started to walk toward the cooler door.

"Put me down! I'm not going any-
where with you!" another mysterious
voice shouted.

Jack froze in his tracks. He looked
nervously around the room. "Hey, who's
that?" he asked. "Is this room haunted, or
what?"

"Jack, I'm the ghost of George
Washington," the second voice said.
"If you make me leave the White House,
I will haunt you forever."

Jack's knees started knocking. He
swallowed hard. "G-g-ghooost?" Jack
stuttered. "I don't see any ghooost."

"Oh, but you will," the voice said.

Suddenly, there was a loud crash! A
flower pot had mysteriously fallen from
the highest shelf. As Jack looked up in
amazement, the ghost said, "Jaaack, I'm
coming to get youuuu."

"I'm out of here!" Jack shouted.

Jack dropped George's portrait like a
hot potato, flung open the cooler door,
and streaked through the florist shop

faster than lightning.

Soon Jack would be outdoors. Soon he would be safe. Or would he?

When Jack pushed the back door open, he saw Big John's truck. Jack smiled. He was almost home free.

Then, without any warning, *Thump!* Jack fell to the ground. "Ouch!" he cried, holding his head.

Jack struggled to get back up. But before he could get on his feet he was hit over the head with one of the world's most dangerous weapons.

Crack! Jack's head felt like it had been split in two. "Owww," he moaned, before slumping over, then passing out cold.

Big John, who was waiting in the truck, saw all the action. But what he didn't see were the FBI agents hiding in the bushes. Before he had a chance to escape, they surrounded his truck. Big John didn't want to end up like Jack, so he surrendered peacefully.

Operation Rescue was a success!

Now that the criminals had been caught and George's portrait was rescued, it was time to say good-bye to the President.

Chapter 17

A Farewell Surprise

When we entered the Oval Office, the President said, "Quick! Everyone sit down. I have lots of questions that need to be answered."

I was worried, and my P.I.s were, too. Was the President disappointed with *Operation Rescue?*

"Mr. President, is something wrong?" I asked.

"Yes!" he exclaimed. "I can't figure out who was the first mysterious voice. The voice of Jack's conscience. And it's driving me crazy!" he said.

Everyone laughed.

Then Birdie, Wally, Sydney, and I pointed toward Mel and shouted, "He's the one!"

"Mr. President, I was the first mysterious voice," Mel said. "I was Jack's conscience."

"What a performance!" the President exclaimed. "But, Mel, how on earth did you know so much about Jack's mother?"

Mel grinned. "Oh, that was easy. When Jack asked a question, Edward told me the answer."

"What?" the President said. "I thought Edward was gagged."

"Oh, he was," Mel agreed. "That's why Jack couldn't hear Edward's answers."

"But you could?" the President asked, sounding confused.

"Yes, Mr. President," Mel replied. "Edward spoke into a special microphone that only I could hear through

127

my earphones. So when Jack asked a question about his mother, Edward would tell me the answer. Then I'd repeat it to Jack."

The President shook his head. "Incredible. Absolutely incredible," he said. "Congratulations, Mel."

"Thank you, Mr. President," Mel replied, beaming.

"MAX, if Mel was the voice of Jack's conscience," the President said, "then who was the voice of George Washington's ghost?"

"Ooooh, I was the ghoooost of George Washington," Birdie answered.

The President laughed loudly. "Great job, Birdie. I especially liked the part when you dropped the flower pot. That really scared Jack."

"It really scared me, too!" Birdie admitted. "It wasn't part of the plan. I accidentally hit it."

The President chuckled. "Well, thank goodness it happened."

The President glanced toward Wally and Sydney. "And thank goodness for the two of you," he said. "Wally, exactly what did you do that made Jack fall down?"

"I gave him one of my famous karate kicks," Wally answered. "I hold a black belt in karate."

"Whoa! I'm impressed," the President replied.

"Don't be impressed," said Wally. "I didn't kick hard enough, so Sydney had to finish the job."

"Sydney?" the President asked.

I knew what the President was thinking: *Sydney, this frail, feminine squirrel? Impossible!*

Oh, if he only knew the truth!

"Mr. President," I said, "Sydney hit Jack over the head with a *very* dangerous weapon."

"She did? What was the weapon?" he asked.

"Show him, Syd," I suggested.

Sydney raised her right leg in the air, and pointed toward her red high heel.

"Ohhh, that does look dangerous," the President remarked. "No wonder Big John surrendered peacefully. He didn't want to tangle with Sydney."

Birdie, Wally, Mel, and I agreed!

"MAX, now that you've captured the criminals and George is back where he belongs, I still don't know who painted the fake portrait."

"Jack did," I answered.

"Jack McDiver?" the President said.

"Yes, Jack McDiver," I replied. "When Jack was living in Paris he studied art. Jack is a very talented painter. But like so many artists, he wasn't receiving a lot of money for his paintings."

"MAX, was Jack planning to sell George's portrait?"

I nodded and answered, "Yes, he had planned to take the portrait out of the country and sell it illegally for millions of dollars."

"MAX, one final question. If Jack and Edward are twin brothers, why is one named Edward Smith and the other is named Jack McDiver?"

"Mr. President, when Jack moved to France, he thought Smith sounded too much like an American name. So Jack changed his last name from Smith to McDiver."

"But why McDiver?" he asked.

Before I could answer the President's question, he shouted, "Wait! Now I remember. Edward's middle name is McDiver."

"Right you are," I replied.

"Well, MAX, I guess that's it," the President said. "All my questions are answered and George is back in the East Room, safe and sound, where he belongs. How can I ever thank you for solving the case of the missing President?"

I smiled. "Mr. President, there's no need to thank me. That's what friends are for. Now I hope you don't mind, but I need to return to Australia tonight."

"Not so fast," the President said. "MAX, I have a surprise for you."

Just then a White House waiter entered with a covered platter of food.

Uh-oh. I recognized the smell. Yuck!

"A little birdie told me this was your favorite late-night snack," the President said as he lifted the cover.

132

"Surprise, MAX! It's pizza with pineapple and anchovies!"

Turn the page to learn about
MAX's V.I.K. Club!

MAX's V.I.K.
(Very Important Kid)
Club!

Mate, if you want to become an exclusive member of my **V.I.K.** Club, you need to send me the following information:

1. Your name
2. Your age
3. Your address (street, state, zip code)
4. Which mystery book you read
5. What you liked best about the book

Send your information to the address below. To learn more information about my V.I.K. Club, check out my fun Web site at **www.maxvikfunpage.com**. Thanks, Mate!

MAX
23015 Del Lago Drive
Suite D2-172
Laguna Hills, California 92653

MAX'S FAN MAIL

Mate, to learn about my books, check out my Web site at **www.maxbooks.com** and for awesome V.I.K. fun, log on to my other site at **www.maxvikfunpage.com**. Thanks for traveling with me. I hope to hear from you.

Your friend,

MAX

j624.2   5719
Strauss
c.1   Chester, Michael
      Joseph Strauss,
      Builder of the Golden
      Gate Bridge

DATE DUE	BORROWER'S NAME	ROOM NUMBER

JOSEPH STRAUSS
BUILDER OF THE
Golden Gate Bridge

Twenty year had passed since Joseph Strauss sat in O'Shaughnessy's office and heard the big red-faced city engineer say, "Why don't you design a bridge for the Golden Gate? Everyone says it can't be done." On May 27, 1937, the Golden Gate Bridge was opened. Joseph Strauss had proved it could be done.

The bridge spanned 4,200 feet of water and was the longest suspension bridge at that time. As a child Strauss had dreamed of doing something that no other man had done. His California bridge was both his ambition and his memorial.

JOSEPH STRAUSS

BUILDER OF THE

Golden Gate Bridge

by Michael Chester

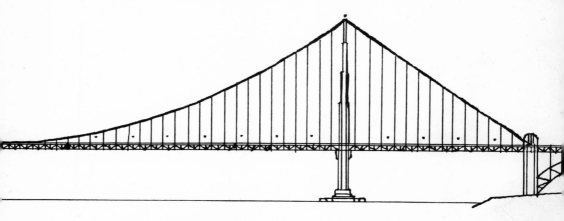

Historical Consultants:
GEORGE R. STEWART
EDNA B. ZIEBOLD, DEPT. OF ED., SAN DIEGO

G. P. PUTNAM'S SONS   NEW YORK

© 1965 by Michael Chester
All Rights Reserved
Published simultaneously in the Dominion of
Canada by Longmans Canada Limited, Toronto
Library of Congress Catalog Card Number: 65-20708
PRINTED IN THE UNITED STATES OF AMERICA
10212

CONTENTS

Golden Gate Bridge

PART ONE

CHAPTER ONE

THE GOLDEN GATE

THE ENTRANCE TO the San Francisco Bay is a channel of water that runs between the cliffs of San Francisco to the south and the cliffs of Marin County to the north. That channel is one of the most beautiful scenes in the world. It is called the Golden Gate.

One million years ago, the entire Bay area was a high, rugged land of wooded mountains. There was no Golden Gate. But two rivers, the Sacramento and the San Joaquin, joined together to empty into the Pacific. Gradually, they wore away a channel to the sea. Then, during the past million years, the land in the Bay area began to break up into great blocks. Some of these blocks rose to form the coastal mountain ridges. Others sank to form the lowlands. The sea poured through the river channel into those lowlands, and, in the course of time, the channel became the Golden Gate, while the lowlands became San Francisco Bay.

The California Indians knew the Golden Gate and the San Francisco Bay long before the Europeans came to the new

world. Even with the sailing ships of Spain and England exploring the California coast, the Golden Gate went undiscovered for a long time. The great English buccaneer and admiral, Sir Francis Drake, sailed along the San Francisco coast in his ship *The Golden Hinde* in 1579, but it seems that he did not see the Golden Gate. From a ship at sea, on a misty day, the Golden Gate would not look different from any of the smaller bays and inlets along the coast. Historians think that Drake landed several miles to the north, where he found a bay and a harbor, later to be known as Drake's Bay. Drake left a bronze plate nailed to a post on the shore. On the plate was engraved Queen Elizabeth's claim to the land. The plate was lost for centuries, later to be found accidentally, after almost four hundred years, in the 1930's on a California beach.

The Spanish were the main explorers of the California coast, but their ships, under the command of such captains as Cermeño and Vizcaino, also missed the Golden Gate, so that the bay went undiscovered.

When the discovery finally came, it was by land. Spanish explorers traveling northward from their settlements in Mexico and San Diego finally reached the great body of water that is San Francisco Bay. Other Spanish explorers, climbing Grizzly Peak on the east side of the bay, saw the Golden Gate in the distance and beyond it the rocky islands of the Farallones and the boundless Pacific.

When finally the Spanish stood on the northern shore of the San Francisco peninsula and looked across the channel, they saw the tides of the Pacific rushing through the gate, a gigantic surge of waters, crested with whitecaps. On the northern side of the channel, they saw an unknown mountainous land rising out of the mist.

13

A year later, in 1775, the first ship came through the gate, the Spanish ship San Carlos, running before the west wind at the turning of the tide. The next year, while American revolutionaries were signing the Declaration of Independence in Philadelphia three thousand miles away, the Spanish captain De Anza was preparing to build a fort beside the Golden Gate to defend a new Spanish settlement.

The channel was not yet called the Golden Gate. It was given that name in the year 1846 by John Fremont, an American adventurer, who rowed across the Golden Gate with Kit Carson and eleven other riflemen to spike the cannons on the Spanish fort. Thus, the Bearflag revolt was one of the steps in taking California away from Mexico, and preparing it for statehood in the United States.

At the Golden Gate, man had come full circle — this was the end of the old journey. There were no more new lands to be found, except for an island here, a mountain range there. But the westward search had reached its limit. Across the Pacific Ocean was the old world again.

Even though the Golden Gate marked the end of the westward explorations, it was the gateway to a different kind of adventure. Man was once more at the dawn of a new age, an age of the human mind, of the great exploits in art, poetry, and science of the twentieth century. In San Francisco, where the westward voyage ended, where the United Nations was to be born, the end of a past era and the dawn of a new era were symbolized. One can think of the Golden Gate, where those two rocky headlands face each other across a swift, terrible current, as the gateway between past and future.

The Golden Gate is the setting for this story. It is the story of the bridge across the Golden Gate and the story of the man who built that bridge.

CHAPTER TWO

THE BOYHOOD OF JOSEPH STRAUSS

JOSEPH STRAUSS was born in the city of Cincinnati, Ohio, on January 9, 1870. His father, Raphael Strauss, was an artist — a well-known painter of portraits in Cincinnati. Joseph's mother, Caroline, was a talented musician.

Joe Strauss was the youngest of four children. He had an older brother and two older sisters. Not only was he the youngest in his family, but he was small for his age. By the time he was four years old, Joe Strauss was used to being smaller than almost everyone he knew.

The world in which Joe Strauss lived and played as a boy was very different from the world of today. The streets and houses of Cincinnati were lit by gaslight rather than by electric lights. People traveled by horse and buggy rather than by automobile. There were no airplanes, no automatic dishwashers, and no neon signs.

The part of Cincinnati where the Strauss family lived was mostly German. Raphael Strauss had come from Bavaria in Germany, at the age of twenty-four, to start a new life in America. Cincinnati was growing very quickly in those years and was already becoming an important center of culture and industry in the middle west.

Visible from the yard of the Strauss home was a great and beautiful bridge across the Ohio River. The bridge had been designed by a famous father and son — the Roeblings. The Roeblings were famous for having built the first suspension bridges in America — bridges whose roadways were suspended

from large cables. They had built the Brooklyn Bridge and a bridge across the Whirlpool Rapids at Niagara Falls.

All through his boyhood, Joe Strauss lived within sight of the bridge across the Ohio. Its great stone pillars and high towers and graceful cables were very familiar to him, for he had seen them many times. In school, he learned about the Roeblings, and how they had built the suspension bridge across the Ohio River. As he grew older and went to high school, he became interested in science and mathematics. But he did not realize, yet, that science and mathematics were the tools that would some day allow him to build a suspension bridge greater than any that the Roeblings built.

When he graduated from high school, the smallest boy in his class, he went to a graduation party. At the party, all of the graduates were asked about their plans — what did they want to become? When it was Joe Strauss's turn to answer, he hesitated. He was not sure what he wanted to do in the world. Then he said, "I would like to do something that nobody has ever done before."

The next fall, Joe Strauss went to the University of Cincinnati to study engineering. His parents were disappointed. They wanted him to be a minister or a lawyer. Or, because of their own interests in art and music, they would have been glad to see their son study one of those fields. Engineering did not seem to be a very artistic subject.

But Joe Strauss had other ideas. He saw engineering as a way of making great and beautiful things. In the hands of a creative man, engineering could be the trade of an artist, and the structures that an engineer built could be like huge, solid pieces of poetry.

At the age of 19, at the University of Cincinnati, Joe Strauss was still very small — barely five feet tall and weighing about 120 pounds. But there was a bold look in his gray eyes and a frankness about his personality that made an impression on people who met him. His manner was gentle, although there were rare occasions when he could be very angry. These traits of character were to play an important part in his life in the years to come.

CHAPTER THREE

A GAME OF FOOTBALL

ONE SEPTEMBER AFTERNOON, in the year 1889, thirty or forty
men were meeting for football practice. They were students at
the University of Cincinnati, and they were getting ready for
the winter football season. Some of them were new players,
trying to make the college team for the first time. Others were
old regulars from last year's team, ready for another season.
The coach had not arrived yet, so the players tossed a football
around, jogged up and down the field, and did pushups and
other exercises.

Suddenly, a strange little figure in a football uniform came
out of the locker room and walked into the midst of the big
players. It was Joe Strauss.

Strauss's uniform was far too big for him and it looked very
baggy. As he walked onto the field, his cuffs kept slipping over
his ankles, and he had to stop several times to pull them up

again. Small or not, he thought as he pulled up his cuffs for the third time, "I'm going to make this team. Maybe my speed will be enough." He wanted very much to be an athletic hero. And he was willing to fight hard to make the team, no matter how big the other players were.

A tackle and a fullback, who were Indian wrestling on the grass, stopped what they were doing and stared in disbelief as Strauss walked past. A halfback who was practicing a punt caught sight of Strauss, and in his surprise, made a lopsided punt into the bleachers.

The players gathered around Strauss, like huge towers around a small wigwam, and looked down at him. The idea of anyone so small trying out for the team struck them funny. They started to tease him. Joe Strauss smiled and tried to be good-natured about the whole thing, but he did not like it very much.

"Hey, get the ball," someone said to the halfback. "You kicked it into the stands."

"Get it yourself," said the halfback.

It looked as if there might be an argument over the ball, so one player who knew Strauss from a history class said, "Let's use Joe for a ball." Then, flinging one arm around Strauss's waist, he dragged the little player forward as if he were crashing through the line.

The other men thought the idea was pretty funny. Before long, they were running around, carrying Strauss as if he were a football, and handing him off to each other in hidden-ball plays. Strauss tried to get away, but he was overpowered. "Come on, fellas, cut it out," he said, as the fullback handed him to the left end. His pride was hurt, because he had come out to be a hero, and they were making him look silly.

The left end decided to run down the field, carrying Joe Strauss for a touchdown. Strauss, with his face dangling just above the grass, watched in helpless fury as the ten-yard lines flashed by. As the end neared the goal line, a defensive player pretended that he was going to tackle him. The end zig-zagged sharply. As he zigzagged, his ankle turned, and he fell forward on top of Strauss.

When the end stood up, rubbing his aching ankle, Strauss lay stunned on the grass. When the players gathered around, they saw that Strauss was hurt. Suddenly, the big men started to feel very ashamed.

Strauss was taken, badly battered, to the hospital. The captain of the football team came to see him there. "You're a good sport, but you're too darned little for football," said the captain, as he stood beside Strauss's bed, staring at the floor and feeling quite uncomfortable.

Joe Strauss had to agree with the team captain — he was too little for football. For two weeks, he lay in the hospital, recovering from his injuries. During those two weeks, he had time to think things over. He decided then that he would do something big some day. He wanted to do a work of power; he wanted to find a way in which a small man could challenge the great world around him. It seemed to him that a man — any man — was a small creature compared to the great world of earth, sea, and sky that surrounded him. He began to feel that there were giants to conquer — giants far greater than football players. As he thought these things, he kept looking out the window, to the familiar sight of the suspension bridge across the Ohio River — the bridge that he had seen all his life. Somehow, its mighty stone pillars comforted him. Joe Strauss was beginning to understand how he would use his engineering art.

In the years that followed, Strauss developed a great interest in bridges. He saw bridges as powerful and noble structures. He saw a challenge in the problems of bridging rivers and canyons and bays, and he saw that there was a chance for fine art work in the lines of bridges. He studied famous bridges: the great cantilever bridges, such as the Firth of Forth Bridge in Scotland, supported by massive iron ribs; the great suspension bridges, such as the Brooklyn Bridge, with its enormous masonry towers; the great arch bridges, such as the Eads Bridge across the Mississippi River at St. Louis, with its three arches of steel.

During the summers, Strauss had his first practical engineering experience, working as a railroad surveyor. He worked with experienced old surveyors, riding out each morning by train, and then going on foot across fields or up the slopes of hills, to survey the land where new railroads would be built. It was hard work, trudging over rocky ground in the heat of summer, with his surveyor's transit over his shoulder, the sweat pouring down his face, and gnats buzzing around him. But it was good work, too, because, as he listened to the talk of the older men, and as he surveyed canyons where railroad bridges were to be built, and as he lived day by day in the wild countryside, he was getting a feeling for his work as an engineer. All

around him were the rivers and ravines that he hoped to bridge some day. Working by his side were the kind of men who would some day be helping him to build bridges. So, Joseph Strauss worked and watched and listened.

Three years after he was used as a football, Joseph Strauss had come a long way. He was the president of his graduating class and the class poet. His poems were about the gigantic universe and about man, a small, adventurous, daring creature in that gigantic universe. Furthermore, he had earned his degree as a civil engineer. For his graduation paper, he designed a bridge across Bering Straits, connecting North America and

Asia. To this day, nobody has built a bridge across Bering Straits. Perhaps there has been no good reason to build one. But if anyone ever wants to build such a bridge, Strauss's paper would probably be useful. Strauss's ideas on bridges were always sharp and clear and original.

With his love of poetry and his imaginary bridges, Strauss was a dreamer. But his dreams were close to the truth. In years to come he would build the most majestic and beautiful bridge in the world.

CHAPTER FOUR

A CAREER BEGINS

AFTER HIS GRADUATION from the University of Cincinnati in 1892, Joseph Strauss went to look for a job. Jobs were not easy to get that year, particularly for a young engineer just out of college, with no practical experience except for summer surveying jobs. Many engineering companies turned the young engineer away. Finally, he was able to get a job in Trenton, New Jersey, working for the New Jersey Steel and Iron Company, bridge builders. Strauss's job was to draw plans for bridges in the company's drafting room. Here, perhaps, was the first step toward his dream as a builder of mighty bridges. But hard times came, and the company was forced to lay off many of its engineers. Strauss was one of those.

He found a job as a mathematics teacher at the University of Cincinnati. For one year he taught there, once more entering the familiar classrooms and walking along the familiar halls and pathways of the campus. But to Strauss, mathematics was important mainly because it was a tool that would be useful in designing bridges. Also, he had a new responsibility — he had asked his girl friend, May Van, of Cincinnati, to marry him. With a wife and family, Strauss would have reason to move ahead quickly in his career. So, after a year of teaching mathematics, Strauss went out as a married man and got another job with a bridge company.

His new employer was the Brackett Bridge Company of Glendale, Ohio. It was a small company, and Strauss was one of the three engineers on the staff. Those were the days when people traveled mainly by horse-and-buggy. The Brackett Bridge Company specialized in small horse-and-buggy bridges on country roads.

Strauss was the junior member of the three-man engineering staff, and he acted mostly as an assistant to the older men. But after a year, Strauss's boss told him that he was going to be given the task of building a bridge near Cincinnati.

That was good news to Strauss. He was going to be able to build a bridge at last. It was a small thing compared with the glorious structure he had designed for the bridging of the Bering Straits. But this would be a real bridge, of steel and mortar — a bridge that horses and wagons would be driven over. It was a dream come true for Strauss, no matter how small a bridge it was.

When his bridge was finished, Strauss stood before it on the dusty road and watched the first wagons rumble across. He felt as proud as if he had built the Taj Mahal. Now, he felt that his career was started. The Brackett Bridge Company had served its purpose, so far as Strauss was concerned. It was time for him to look for new horizons. He left his job and bought a train ticket for Chicago.

For two years, Strauss held odd jobs for bridge companies in Chicago and in New York, gradually adding to his knowledge of and experience with bridges. Then, finally, at the age of twenty-nine he was hired by the firm of a very famous bridge builder, Ralph Modjeski. The Modjeski company specialized in heavy railroad bridges. "Here," thought Strauss, "is my chance to build some big bridges." But he found himself stuck in an office job, handling business details. He did not have nearly as much to do with the design of bridges as he had hoped.

Now it happened, at that time, that a new kind of movable bridge was becoming popular. The old kind of movable bridge

was the kind that turned sideways rather than upward, moving out of the way of ships like a door on a hinge. These turnstile bridges used too much room in their method of operation. Therefore, engineers were taking an interest in "bascule bridges," which worked like the old-time drawbridges used across the moats of castles.

Bascule bridges had recently become popular in Europe. A bascule bridge could have a single span (single-leaf bascule) or a double span (double-leaf bascule) which would raise to let ships pass. The great Dutch artist Vincent Van Gogh painted his impressions of a small double-leaf bascule bridge across the Rhone, at about the time that Joe Strauss was graduating from high school in Cincinnati. Van Gogh's painting, titled *The Bridge at Arles*, became one of the world's great masterpieces.

Meanwhile, bridge engineers were involved in the more practical problems of constructing large bascule bridges that would bear heavy traffic. There were serious problems in the design of the seesaw mechanism of large bascule bridges. The engineers at the Modjeski company were among those who were working hard on bascule bridge designs.

The span of a bascule bridge is a large, heavy thing — a roadway that may be millions of pounds in weight. When the span is raised, a heavy counterweight must be lowered to balance it. The operation of a bascule bridge is much like the operation of a seesaw. The counterweight of the bridge is like the weight of the person on the low end of the seesaw.

The trouble with bascule bridges was that almost as much iron was needed in the counterweight as in the span itself. The huge weight of iron in the counterweight made it quite costly to build bascule bridges. Engineers at the Modjeski company and elsewhere were wracking their brains to find a way to get efficient counterweight action without having to make such heavy counterweights. But nobody could find any very good answer to the problem.

Strauss was not assigned to the bascule bridge problem. But he worked on the problem in his spare time, and came up with his own original design for a bascule bridge. His design was quite different from the approaches that other engineers had taken. Strauss's design made use of counterweights made of concrete rather than of iron.

One evening, Strauss told another engineer in the company about his plans for a bascule bridge.

"Joe, you can't make your counterweights out of concrete," said the engineer. "It isn't heavy enough."

"Suppose I make the counterweights twice as big or three times as big as the regular iron counterweights. Then they'll be heavy enough."

"Sure," said the engineer. "But they'll be enormous. They won't be able to slide into place without banging into the supports."

Strauss smiled. He had already thought about that problem. He had invented a new kind of mechanism for the moving counterweight — a mechanism that would allow a large concrete weight to move into place without interference.

The next afternoon, Strauss told his other colleagues about his bascule bridge, spreading his engineering drawings over a drafting board, and explaining the details of operation. The other men only shook their heads. They felt that the operation of a bascule bridge was complicated enough without using Strauss's methods. It seemed to them that the money saved in using concrete counterweights was overshadowed by the risks in using a new approach. So far as they were concerned,

Strauss's bascule bridge was a wild design, and they wanted nothing to do with it.

"You'd better stick to managing the office, Joe," said one of the men.

Strauss was bitterly disappointed. He had expected Ralph Modjeski and the other engineers to praise him for his original design. He folded the drawings of his bascule bridge, put them into a briefcase, and strode out the door. He was through with the Modjeski company.

A few days later, in a cramped, dark little office down the street, Strauss opened his own bridge-building business. Over the door of his office, he put a sign, which read:

JOSEPH B. STRAUSS AND COMPANY.

The only trouble was that Joseph B. Strauss and Company had no customers. The question was, how could he get his first customers, now that he was in business for himself? He had something to sell — his new design for a bascule bridge. But would anybody buy a strange, new design from an unknown bridge builder?

When Strauss set out to sell his idea, he found no buyers. Therefore, he decided to enlarge his operation. If he became a bridge contractor, as well as a bridge designer, then he might be able to sell his ideas as part of a construction bid.

Finally, after he had been turned away from the doors of many customers, Strauss made his first big sale. A railroad company agreed to let him build one of his bascule bridges for them in Cleveland. But the railroad men drove a hard bargain. They would not pay Strauss until he had finished the bridge and proved that it worked.

Now Strauss had quite a problem. He had to spend eighty thousand dollars to build his bridge. The railroad company would not give him a dollar until it was finished. Strauss had to borrow the money. Bit by bit, he was able to borrow what he needed. Also, he charged many of the supplies that he bought. When he had scraped together every dollar he could borrow, plus all his own savings, and gone deeply into debt, he was ready to build his bridge.

Strauss was in a difficult situation. If his bridge was not successful, he would lose all the thousands of dollars that he had invested in it, and he would be in debt for many years — perhaps for the rest of his life. Worst of all, he would be a failure in his art of bridge building. But he trusted his own ability. And in his earnest, ambitious manner, he had led other people to trust in him and to lend him the money that he needed so badly. He was determined not to fail.

CHAPTER FIVE

FOUR HUNDRED BRIDGES

JOSEPH STRAUSS was on hand to watch his bridge being built. He checked every step in the construction, to make sure that nothing went wrong. Also, he kept double-checking his own calculations, to make sure that he had made no mistakes. He knew that his future as a bridge builder was riding on the success of his first bascule bridge.

Many railroad men were interested in the new type of bascule bridge that Strauss had designed, and they were on hand to see it in operation on the first day that it opened. "Nothing had better go wrong now," thought Strauss, as he waited for the closing of the bridge. The bridge had been built with its movable span raised, and ships had been moving back and forth along the Cuyahoga River during the morning. Now, with the ceremonies scheduled for noon, the bridge was ready for its big test. There was no reason for anything to go wrong,

39

and Strauss was confident of his own ability. Still, strange things could happen with bridges, and this was a new, untried design.

The speeches of dedication for the bridge were made, and the ceremonies completed. Strauss gave the signal to the man in the control tower. There was a rumble from the powerful motors that sent the counterweight into motion. The span moved downward, dropping into position with a dull metallic ring. The bridge was in operation. A few minutes later, the first locomotive rumbled slowly across the Cuyahoga River. The bridge was a success, and Joseph Strauss knew that he was on his way as a bridge builder.

Soon, Strauss had orders for two more bascule bridges. Both were successful pieces of engineering — one in Rahway, New Jersey, and the other in upstate New York. But, they were not financial successes for Strauss. He still did not know as much about the art of running a business as he did about the art of building bridges. He found that he was earning very little money.

While he was puzzling over his money troubles, Strauss was given a contract for the building of his fourth bridge. This bridge, built for the Elgin-Belvidere Railroad in Illinois, was one of the most difficult tasks Strauss ever tackled.

The concrete foundations that the supports of a bridge rest on are called "piers." In building the Elgin-Belvidere Railroad bridge, Strauss found that he was going to have to build one of the piers in quicksand. To solve the problem, Strauss sank steel frameworks into the quicksand, closing in the quicksand so that it could not flow. The boxed-in quicksand made a firm foundation for the pier. For years afterward, engineers from all over the country came to see the bridge pier that

had been built in quicksand. It was an amazing piece of engineering.

After that, many orders came to the Strauss Company for bridges. Many of them were for bridge jobs so difficult that other bridge companies would have refused them. Strauss built forty bridges in the mountains of Panama — bridges whose parts had to be delivered on the backs of mules. He built a bridge across the Pei-Ho River at Tientsin, China, and had the sayings of Confucius carved into its arches. He built a beautiful double-leafed bascule bridge at the winter palace of the Czar of Russia, across the river Neva.

41

Over the years, Strauss built more than four hundred bridges. Most of them were Strauss bascule bridges, but improved in many ways over the one that he had designed when he was a young engineer at the Ralph Modjeski Company. Strauss's bascule bridges revolutionized the entire art of building movable bridges.

Now, many years had gone by. Joseph Strauss was the father of two boys, and was an experienced professional in the art of bridge building. But he was still the same man in many ways — gentle and soft-spoken most of the time, but fierce, angry, and determined in his work. When any obstacle stood in the way of his bridge building, whether it was a natural obstacle or a human obstacle, Joseph Strauss would fight hard to overcome it. Let someone say that one of his bridge plans was impossible or impractical, and the gentle little bridge builder would be ready to battle. His pride and ambition and force of personality were like furnaces that kept him working into the dead of night pouring all his energy into the bridging of rivers and canyons.

In the year 1917, when Joseph Strauss was forty-seven years old, he made a trip to San Francisco. It was a business trip, on which he had come to talk to Michael M. O'Shaughnessy, the San Francisco city engineer. A number of small bridges were to be built over San Francisco streets, and the Strauss company was bidding on the job.

When the little bridge builder, with his swift, alert gray eyes, stepped out of his train at the San Francisco station, he was facing the greatest challenge of his career. But he did not know it yet.

CHAPTER SIX

AN IMPOSSIBLE ASSIGNMENT

STRAUSS SAT ACROSS the desk from O'Shaughnessy, the big, red-faced city engineer. They had finished their discussions about the bridges for downtown San Francisco. Now they were having a friendly chat before it was time for Strauss to take the train to Chicago.

There was a pause in the conversation, neither man saying anything for several seconds. Strauss was thinking about work that had to be done at the Chicago office. O'Shaughnessy was looking out the window. Then he turned to Strauss and said, with a grin, "Why don't you design a bridge for the Golden Gate? Everybody says it can't be done."

"I think it can," said Strauss. He looked out the window too, over the buildings and hilly streets and cable cars of San Francisco, to San Francisco Bay in the distance.

"It would cost a hundred million dollars," said O'Shaugh-

nessy, "and that's too much." He spoke with an Irish brogue, for he had been born in Limerick, Ireland, and had not come to America until the age of twenty-one.

"How much will the job stand?" asked Strauss.

"Twenty-five or thirty million dollars at the most."

"All right," said Strauss, "if you have soundings made in the channel, I'll see what I can do for you."

O'Shaughnessy raised his eyebrows. He was not sure that Strauss could bridge the Golden Gate for such a low cost. But he suspected that Strauss could, if anyone could. O'Shaughnessy agreed to have soundings made of the channel, so that the depths and the nature of the rocky bottom could be known.

O'Shaughnessy had good reasons for his doubts. At its narrowest, the Golden Gate was a mile wide, and the currents through it were strong and treacherous. It was a channel that would make trouble for any bridge maker — even a bridge maker as good as Joseph Strauss.

There are many ways to make a bridge. The kind of bridge that an engineer designs depends a great deal on how he decides to support the roadway. The roadway of a bridge is called a "span," and the foundations that support the span are called

piers. But there are several ways in which a span can be supported on the piers. Large, modern bridges can generally be divided into four different kinds, depending on how the span is supported. These four kinds of bridges are truss bridges, arch bridges, cantilever bridges, and suspension bridges.

A good example of a truss bridge is the Sciotoville Bridge across the Ohio River between Ohio and Kentucky. The Sciotoville Bridge is 1,550 feet long, and rests on three concrete piers, one at either shore, and one in the middle of the Ohio River. If the Sciotoville Bridge were made of long, solid bars of steel, it would sag in the spaces between the piers and collapse under its own weight. But a truss is not a solid bar of steel — instead, it

is a skeleton of steel with crisscross ribs. A truss is almost as strong as a solid bar of steel, but much lighter. Therefore, it is strong enough and light enough to support its own weight quite well. The crisscross metal ribs of the Sciotoville Bridge form a single, gigantic truss, stretching from one side of the river to the other, and resting on the three piers.

If the Golden Gate were a shallow channel with gentle tides, an engineer might decide to build a row of several piers all the way across the channel. Then, a truss span could rest on the piers. But in order to bridge the Golden Gate, it was clear that the supports would have to be built near each shore. It would be impossible to rest a span on piers built near each shore, without support in the middle: the center of the bridge would collapse, even if it were the strongest of trusses.

Arch bridges have been used for thousands of years. The first people to build arch bridges were the ancient Romans. By cementing stones or bricks into the shape of an arch, Roman engineers were able to make very strong structures to hold up their bridges. In modern times, steel arches are used.

The reader can carry out a simple experiment to see how an arch holds up a bridge. Use two books as piers, and a playing card (or a postcard or other piece of cardboard) as a span, placing the card so that its ends are supported by the edges of the books. If you put a weight on the card, for instance a stone, the card will buckle in the middle. But you can make a stronger bridge if you bend the card into a curved bow, and use the two books to block the ends, so that the card cannot straighten. Now, the card is like an arch "sprung" between two piers. You can put much more weight on the arched card than you could on the straight card, without buckling it.

Like the card arched between the books, an arch is "sprung"

47

between the piers of the bridge, or, in some cases, between towers that are built on the piers. The arch pushes outward against the piers. The span can either rest on top of the arch, or it can hang below the arch. But an arch bridge a mile long was out of the question. That ruled out an arch bridge for the Golden Gate.

A cantilever bridge uses two kinds of span. The side spans of the bridge are called "cantilever spans." They jut out from either shore, resting on the supporting piers, and heavily braced by steel towers. Then a center span is rested across the ends of the two cantilever spans. The weight of the suspended span is balanced by the downward force on the cantilever spans where they are attached to the great masses of concrete at the anchorages.

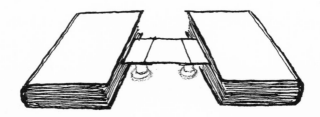

Strauss felt that a cantilever bridge measuring a mile between piers could not be built. That left only the suspension bridge. A suspension bridge is held up by steel cables strung between a pair of towers. The span is suspended from the steel cables. When Strauss started to think about bridging the Golden Gate, the most famous suspension bridge in the world was the Brooklyn Bridge, crossing the East River between Brooklyn and Manhattan. John Roebling, who designed the Brooklyn Bridge, made the building of suspension bridges into a great art. He was killed during the early work on the Brooklyn Bridge, and his son, Washington Roebling, carried on the task in his place, building the bridge in his father's design.

The suspended span of the Brooklyn Bridge stretches about 1,600 feet between the two towers. When it was completed in 1883, it was the longest suspension span in the world. Many bridge engineers felt that the Brooklyn Bridge was as long as any suspension span should be, and that a much longer suspension span would collapse. The mile-wide Golden Gate channel would need a span many times longer. That seemed impossible. Suspension bridges longer than the Brooklyn Bridge just were not being built.

Now, whether a bridge is a truss, an arch, a cantilever, or a suspension bridge, its two ends must be supported by piers. At the Golden Gate, the piers would have to be built on the floor of the channel, no matter what kind of bridge was built. The

building of bridge piers in the channel was the big problem. That was the problem that made Michael O'Shaughnessy shake his head and knit his shaggy eyebrows. That was the problem that rose as a great challenge to Strauss as he awaited the results on the soundings of the channel. But even without the soundings, everyone knew that the Golden Gate was a very wide, deep, treacherous place to build bridge piers. Perhaps the task was impossible.

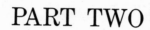

PART TWO

CHAPTER SEVEN

YEARS OF STRUGGLE

ALTHOUGH STRAUSS did not know it, O'Shaughnessy had been talking with a number of bridge engineers about the Golden Gate problem. The bridging of the Golden Gate was an old idea, and it had come up a number of times in the past. But people seemed to think that it was a wild idea, and not at all practical. Still, the counties to the north, Marin, Sonoma, Napa, and Solano, were isolated from the San Francisco peninsula. The ferry boats were slow and crowded, and the northern counties were growing in population. Many people in cities such as San Rafael in Marin County and Santa Rosa in Sonoma County worked in San Francisco. The need for a bridge was growing all the time.

O'Shaughnessy was moving slowly and carefully. He was not going to rush into a costly project, without knowing exactly where he was going. He knew that the decision as to whether or not the bridge should be built was a political decision that would depend on the voters of the San Francisco Bay area. In fact, the next step was a political one. The San Francisco City Council would have to ask the U.S. Government Coast and Geodetic Survey to carry out the channel soundings.

It was a few years after Strauss and O'Shaughnessy first talked about the bridge before the soundings were taken. The soundings showed that the rock bottom of the channel was 250 feet below the surface, at its deepest. On the north side of the channel, near Marin, the channel dropped off sharply, becoming deep very quickly. The north pier of the bridge would therefore have to be built close to the Marin shore.

The slope on the south side of the channel was gentle. For more than a thousand feet from the San Francisco shore, the water was less than a hundred feet deep. Therefore, the south pier could be built some distance from shore, in order to make the distance between the towers as short as possible. But even with the south pier a thousand feet from shore, the distance between the towers would still be more than 4,000 feet.

Even though Strauss was an imaginative, daring bridge builder, he was also very careful. He did not believe that a suspension bridge more than 4,000 feet long could be built. He was one of those engineers who felt that the 1,600-foot span of the Brooklyn Bridge was about the limit in suspension bridges. Strauss spent long nights in his Chicago office, struggling to design a bridge that could span the broad channel. Finally, he decided on a combination bridge — part cantilever and part suspension. The suspended span would be held up partly by two great steel cantilever arms, and partly by cables strung between the cantilever towers. Strauss called his design a "symmetrical cantilever suspension bridge." Late in 1921, he submitted his bid for the contract. He estimated that the bridging of the Golden Gate would cost seventeen million dollars. Strauss's bid was the lowest bid made. Only one other engineer had placed a bid. The other bid was from Gustav Lindenthal of New York, who estimated that it would cost fifty-six million dollars for the bridge. Strauss's plans seemed to offer the best practical solution to the bridging of the Golden Gate.

Strauss, O'Shaughnessy, and other men who favored the bridge joined together to win public support for the project. For Strauss, the year 1922 was a year of public speeches and private meetings in San Francisco, as he worked hard to convince people that the Golden Gate Bridge could be built, and should be built. He found many people who liked the idea. He also found people who did not like the idea at all. The opponents of the bridge idea felt that it would be impossible to build a strong, safe bridge across the deep channel, or that it would cost too much money, or that the bridge would ruin the appearance of the beautiful Golden Gate channel.

Strauss believed in his bridge, and fought hard against his opponents, explaining how the bridge would be built, and how it would be strengthened to resist the forces of wind and tide. He also explained how a toll gate on the bridge would take care of cost problems over the years. He told people how a bridge can be a work of art, adding to the beauty and power of a natural scene.

By the end of 1922, many people were interested in the building of the Golden Gate Bridge. The hard year's work that Strauss, O'Shaughnessy, and the other men had spent in San Francisco, talking and arguing until they were hoarse, had finally brought results. Newspapers and business organizations were taking a strong interest in the bridge.

Those were days of political struggle, days in which Strauss was surrounded by towering men who took one side or the other in the fight for the bridge, while Strauss himself stood among them, a head shorter than they, but fighting for all he was worth.

Sometimes, after such days, he would go to the Golden Gate. He would stand at Fort Point, by the old brick walls and gun rests of the historic fort, looking out over the water he had to conquer. On the rocks nearby stood fishermen casting their lines over the choppy waters. The sea slapped against the rocks, hurling up fountains of white spray. Out in the middle of the channel, when the tide was going out, Strauss could see the terrible current rushing toward the Pacific, carrying whitecaps and bits of driftwood westward. Across the channel, he could see Lime Point, on the Marin shore. As he watched this wild scene and listened to the screeches of the gulls, Strauss could imagine the bridge that he would build from Fort Point to Lime Point. The fishermen would have been amazed, if they could have seen the vision of steel and concrete that Strauss saw as he stood by the Golden Gate, staring into the future.

CHAPTER EIGHT

THE WAR DEPARTMENT AND THE BRIDGE

THE UNITED STATES WAR DEPARTMENT would not allow any bridge to be built that would in any way weaken the great naval port of San Francisco Bay. During the years of argument about the Golden Gate Bridge, investigations were held by the War Department. The War Department was interested in two questions: would the bridge block the channel, keeping high-masted warships from entering? or, if the bridge were destroyed by an earthquake or by enemy action during a war, would its wreckage block the channel? These questions were vital to the strength of the U.S. Navy's Pacific fleet.

In one meeting, Strauss and O'Shaughnessy spoke before a board of inquiry in San Francisco, explaining that the bridge would be high enough to allow room for those warships that had the highest masts. They also pointed out that, on the latest ships being built, the masts were smaller. Also, the lights on the piers and towers of the bridge would mark the channel, and would be useful navigation aides for ships as they went in and out of San Francisco Bay.

But Strauss's opponents spoke at the War Department hearings too. In one of the hearings, Strauss explained that the height of the bridge above the water would change. Sometimes it would be as great as 236 feet. At other times it would be only 220 feet.

"You mean," said the lawyer who was questioning him, "that the clearance will be sixteen feet greater at low tide than at high tide?"

"No," said Strauss. "What I mean is that the cables lengthen on hot days and lower the bridge sixteen feet."

The lawyer smiled. Since he represented people who were against the building of the bridge, his job was to make Strauss look foolish. "Oh," he said, "so you are building a rubber bridge, are you?"

Many of the people in the hearing laughed at the lawyer's joke. But Strauss explained to them how metal expands or contracts, depending on its temperature.

Other questions were asked, and there was some discussion. But there was very little argument, and the military men seemed to be satisfied with what they had heard. The hearing lasted for three hours. After it was over, O'Shaughnessy and Strauss left feeling that they had won another victory.

But the Government moves slowly sometimes. Strauss and O'Shaughnessy had to wait all year to get the final decision of the War Department. On December 20, 1924, the decision was made. The War Department had no objections to the proposed Golden Gate Bridge.

The State of California and the United States War Department had given their permission for the formation of a bridge district and the building of the bridge. But they were not the only ones who had to agree. The counties of the bay area had to pass ordinances for the formation of a bridge district. The people of the bay area counties were the ones who would have to pay the taxes for a bridge, and therefore the county boards of supervisors would have to vote on the issue.

Strauss's estimate for the building of the bridge was now twenty-one million dollars, because the cost of building bridges had changed since his original estimate in 1921. But now he guaranteed that the total cost of the bridge would be within ten percent of his twenty-one million dollar estimate. Reassured by Strauss's statement, the San Francisco Board of Supervisors voted unanimously, in April of 1925, to form a bridge district. By November, five other bay area counties had joined the district.

Eight long years had gone by since O'Shaughnessy first asked Strauss about bridging the Golden Gate. During those years, the two men had fought hard for the idea. Now, finally, the building of the bridge seemed close. Strauss and O'Shaughnessy did not know that there would be another eight years of political struggle before the work could start.

CHAPTER NINE

THE ATTACK ON STRAUSS

IN NOVEMBER 1927, the opponents of the bridge began to attack Strauss. They claimed that Strauss was an outsider who was trying to deceive the people of San Francisco. They also said that he was not a good engineer, and that his ideas on bridge design were unsound.

In the town of Santa Rosa, on the California coast to the north of the Golden Gate, the attack on Strauss became public. The opponents of the bridge formed a group called the "Taxpayers' Protective League," in order to protest against the building of the bridge. Public hearings opened in Santa Rosa on the first day of November. The Taxpayers' League brought engineers into court to prove that the bridge should not be built.

The engineers who testified had many criticisms to make. One of their main complaints was about the rock at the bottom of the channel where the south pier was to be built. The engineers said that the rock was weak and crumbling. Also, they said, the San Andreas earthquake fault lay only five miles west of the Golden Gate. The motion of the rocks of the fault had caused the great San Francisco earthquake of 1906. What would happen to the Golden Gate Bridge if the San Andreas acted up again?

But throughout the hearing, the angriest attacks were those made on Strauss. "Just who is this little man who thinks he's so big?" asked Strauss's opponents. In every way that they could, they tried to show that Strauss knew very little about bridges.

Strauss was not in Santa Rosa to defend himself. He was working in his Chicago office, while his opponents attacked him in the courtroom. But other members of the Golden Gate Bridge Association decided that he should be there to defend himself. So they asked him to come to San Francisco immediately. Dropping all other work, Strauss rushed to San Francisco. On Friday, November 4, he was in Santa Rosa.

Everyone knew that the most important part of the hearing was ready to begin, as they watched Strauss walk calmly forward to take the stand. George H. Harlan, a very skillful lawyer, was standing by to help Strauss defend the bridge. With George Harlan asking questions, Strauss explained his plans. He told the court that, from the soundings taken by the U.S. Coast and Geodetic Survey, there was no reason to doubt the bedrock at the south pier site. As to an earthquake — an earthquake big enough to destroy the bridge would be big enough to destroy the city of San Francisco. But there was no reason to think that another big earthquake would strike San Francisco. Even though he defended the bridge that he was planning,

Strauss did not say a great deal to defend himself against the personal attacks that had been made on him.

Then, the lawyer for the Taxpayers' League started the cross-examination. For three hours, he questioned Strauss, sometimes shouting at him. But Strauss stayed calm and confident. The lawyer tried to give the impression that Strauss's interest in the bridge was entirely selfish. "Mr. Strauss," he asked, "you did this work in expectation of being made the district engineer — did you not?"

Strauss was not bothered by that question. He answered, "Most certainly." He saw no reason to deny that he was interested in the position of chief engineer.

65

Throughout the three hours Strauss defended himself calmly and with great confidence, as the lawyer for the Taxpayers' League bombarded him with loud, angry questions. Sometimes Strauss refused to answer questions because, he said, the questions were illogical. By the time the long cross-examination was ended it was clear to everyone that Strauss had defended himself well.

The next day, the hearings continued. Professor Wing of Stanford University was called to the stand to testify. He called Strauss's ideas "wild guessing" and "ridiculous." Later, when Strauss was called to the stand again, he quietly pointed out that "Professor Wing has not made a very careful check on the design. . . ."

After Strauss talked, other members of the Golden Gate Bridge Association spoke in favor of the bridge. Finally, the hearing was ended. The judge found the Golden Gate Bridge District to be useful and beneficial. Strauss had won. The bridge district was legal. The Golden Gate Bridge Association, which had fought for so many years in favor of the bridge, would now be dissolved. The bridge district would now carry on the work of building the bridge..

Before the work could begin, the new district would have to choose its leaders. One of the most important positions was the position of chief engineer. Strauss was a logical choice for chief engineer. He had spent years in planning and struggling to bridge the Golden Gate. He knew more than anyone else about the subject, and he was the only man who had offered a plan at a reasonable cost.

But the angry, determined little bridge builder had made enemies. Many people felt that he was too proud and too quick to say what he thought. Some of those people said that another chief engineer should be chosen.

In order to be fair to everyone, the leaders of the bridge district talked to several engineers who could have served as chief engineer on the Golden Gate Bridge. But after all the engineers had been considered, it was clear that Joseph B. Strauss was by far the best man for the job. So, in spite of what some people thought, the leaders of the district chose Strauss as chief engineer for the building of the Golden Gate Bridge.

CHAPTER TEN

THE SOUTH PIER BATTLE

WHILE THE BRIDGE DISTRICT was still looking for a way to pay for the cost of building the bridge, Strauss was impatient. He was so impatient that he was willing to spend his own money to study the building problems that he would face. So he hired experts, including a consulting geologist from the University of California, Andrew G. Lawson. Professor Lawson was to study the problems of building a pier on the bedrock near the south shore of the channel. Meanwhile, Strauss started to make a general engineering and traffic study. All of the money for the studies was supplied by the Strauss Bascule Bridge Company.

The building of the south pier, 1,100 feet off the south shore of the channel, in strong ocean currents where the water was a hundred feet deep, was the biggest challenge that Strauss faced. Also, he wanted to quiet the rumors that the bedrock was weak and crumbling. For these reasons, Strauss was deeply interested in the south pier study. Divers were hired to investigate the bedrock.

During the survey, a deep-sea diver came up with bad news. After his helmet had been taken off, he said that the bedrock where the south pier was to be built was as "soft as plum pudding."

Strauss and other engineers questioned the diver to find out whether he was sure of what he had seen. The diver nodded, as assistants helped him out of his heavy suit. "There are mermaid's caverns down there too," he said.

The diver's report on the soft rock and his joke about the mermaid's caverns caused Strauss a great deal of trouble. Nobody wanted to sink a bridge pier into soft rock that was full of caverns, mermaids or no mermaids. Strauss had other divers sent down, again and again, to explore the bedrock. Hundreds of holes were drilled into the rock, over an area ten acres in size. Nothing was found but hard serpentine rock. The "plum pudding" rock reported by the lone diver was never located.

But the trouble caused by the plum-pudding report did not go away so easily. A committee of three geologists was asked to report on the bedrock for the south pier. Two of the geologists, Andrew Lawson and Allan Sedgwick, gave a favorable report. But the third geologist, Robert A. Kinzie of San Francisco, disagreed. He quoted the diver's report on the soft rock and the caverns. Was it safe to build a bridge on that kind of foundation in a place with a history of earthquakes? Robert Kinzie did not think so.

Someone asked Strauss what he thought of Kinzie's remarks. At the time, Strauss was surveying the Golden Gate. He pointed toward old Fort Point and the sea wall below it on the south shore of the channel. "In eighty years, earthquakes haven't broken those walls," he said.

70

There were other rumors about the south pier site. Some critics claimed that the pier site was at the edge of a steep drop in the floor of the channel. During the year 1934, Strauss and Professor Bailey Willis of Stanford University were to argue this question many times over.

Bailey Willis, a retired professor of geology, claimed that Strauss was getting ready to build the south pier practically on the edge of an underwater cliff. He also spoke a great deal about the earthquake hazard and about the "mermaid's caverns."

Strauss and the other engineers of the bridge district struck back with hard questions: had Professor Willis examined the bedrock in person? had he studied the survey that Strauss was conducting? if he had not done either of these things, how did he get his information about the bedrock?

Of course, everyone knew that Professor Willis, an elderly man, had not gone underwater in a diving suit to examine the bedrock. Professor Willis admitted that he had not examined the bedrock, nor had he studied Strauss's survey. But he had a Coast Guard map showing the underwater cliff at the pier site.

But Strauss and the other engineers were able to show that Professor Willis was using an outdated map which had large errors in measurement. After that, the arguments about the bedrock quieted down. But the arguments did their damage; real or unreal, the mermaid's caverns, and the earthquakes, and the underwater cliffs caused serious money problems for Strauss, as will be shown in the next chapter.

CHAPTER ELEVEN

THE COST OF A BRIDGE

THIRTY-FIVE MILLION DOLLARS — that was the money needed, if the Golden Gate Bridge were to be built. The cost of labor and materials had increased during the past five years. The counties of the bay area would have to borrow that money from the banks, and would have to pay it back with interest. The taxpayers were not too happy about having to pay the interest on thirty-five million dollars. But Strauss and the other members of the bridge district argued that tolls would more than make up for the interest. In the long run, they said, the taxpayers would not lose money.

In 1930, there was an election to decide whether the thirty-five million dollars should be borrowed. The citizens of the bay area counties would have to vote on the loan, and a two-thirds majority would be needed to pass it.

There was a great deal of argument about the loan. Many

people thought that the citizens would be better off if they voted against the loan bonds. During the months before the bond election, Strauss's old friend, M. M. O'Shaughnessy, had a change of heart. He said to Strauss, "Your bridge is all right, but you can never convince people it can be built." Finally, O'Shaughnessy decided to argue against the bonds. As city engineer of San Francisco, he felt that the public could not afford to back the bonds. Times were changing, and O'Shaughnessy was not at all sure that the bonds could be sold to the banks. Therefore, Strauss and O'Shaughnessy, who once had fought side by side to bridge the Golden Gate, found themselves on opposite sides.

When the election came in November 1930, there was a large vote in favor of the bonds. A cartoon in a San Francisco newspaper showed crowds of people celebrating the passage of the bond issue, while O'Shaughnessy walked away, sad and alone.

In Santa Rosa, people were overjoyed. On the Thursday night following the election, crowds gathered to celebrate. It was a chilly evening, and huge bonfires were built. Bands played, and speeches were made. One of the speakers was Joseph B. Strauss. A tremendous cheer rose from the crowd, as the little engineer stood before the microphone. "They have told you the bridge can't be built," said Strauss. "You believed those who told you it could be built." He also promised his audience that there would be many jobs, when the building of the bridge began. In those hard times, that was good news.

But, because the early 1930's were hard times, the banks were not in a hurry to buy the bonds. They were not at all sure that the bonds were a good investment. It was all very well that people had voted in favor of borrowing the thirty-five million dollars. But who would lend it?

Strauss was desperate. He decided to visit Mr. A. P. Giannini of the Bank of America. A. P. Giannini was one of the most powerful men in California. And he was known for his daring and his farsightedness. He listened as Strauss presented his case. Strauss told him of the long years of struggle. And Strauss talked, too, about the bridge, and why he felt that it should be built. A. P. Giannini listened, and asked a few questions, which Strauss answered. And then the banker said, "San Francisco needs that bridge. We'll take the bonds."

The money troubles were not ended. Those were the years of the great depression in America. Millions of people were out of work, and money was scarce. After buying a first bond issue of six million dollars, the Bank of America had to stop buying bonds.

Meanwhile, Strauss was having arguments with people on how the bridge district should spend the six million dollars. There were differences of opinion on details of bridge construction. In a meeting on some of these problems, Strauss had a sharp quarrel with his former friend, M. M. O'Shaughnessy. O'Shaughnessy suggested that Strauss did not know what he was doing.

Angered by this attack on his skill as an engineer, Strauss reminded O'Shaughnessy that he was the designer of the Strauss bascule bridge, the most technical bridge in engineering. He suggested that O'Shaughnessy did not know enough about engineering to understand a Strauss bascule bridge.

O'Shaughnessy jumped to his feet. "How come a Strauss bridge fell down in New Jersey last year?" he shouted. "And all the owners had left was a bunch of lawsuits."

"I am sorry that Mr. O'Shaughnessy is obliged to make discourteous remarks," said Strauss to the people at the meeting

table. Then, turning to the furious city engineer, he said, "A bridge, Mr. O'Shaughnessy, must be maintained like any other piece of machinery, and in this instance, the maintenance was not up to the Strauss Company, but to the owners."

The two men who had stood side by side through so many years were now far apart. Their quarrel was not to last too long, because a year later M. M. O'Shaughnessy was dead, at the age of seventy. Strauss remembered the times when he and O'Shaughnessy had worked together. Years later, when the Golden Gate Bridge had been built, Strauss wrote an article for the *Saturday Evening Post,* telling the long story of how the bridge was fought for and how it was built. His article was titled: "Here Is Your Bridge, Mr. O'Shaughnessy."

Other struggles blocked Strauss's way during the early 1930's. During the years of depression, still unable to sell the bridge bonds, the bridge district applied for a loan from the Government of the United States. But that was the time when Professor Bailey Willis was arguing strongly about the bedrock at the south pier site. It was because of that argument that the United States Government was unwilling to finance the building of the bridge.

During those years, Strauss was still spending his own money on plans and surveys for the bridge. Perhaps he remembered how he had risked so much money in the building of his first bascule bridge, and how he had won. While he was waiting for funds to bridge the Golden Gate, he spent a quarter of a million dollars of his own money. Also, he spent countless hours of his own time, riding the train between Chicago and San Francisco, spending his time sketching piers, towers, and cables, or writing poems, as the train sped across the prairies and deserts and wound through mountain passes. He looked out with a skillful, critical eye at the bridges that the train crossed, perhaps recognizing some of them as his own.

From the San Francisco station, he would go to his offices at 901 Sutter Street. There, nine stories above the traffic of downtown San Francisco, he sketched, and planned, and calculated. During those hours, on sheets of paper, he was already conquering the waters of the Golden Gate as they rushed into the Pacific with the outgoing tide.

Finally, times were better. The Bank of America had recovered, and was operating again at full strength. The sale of bonds to the bank continued, and there was no longer anything to stop Strauss from building his bridge — nothing, that is, but the forces of wind and tide. But Joseph Strauss was sure that he could conquer those obstacles. He was the builder of more than four hundred bridges, and had conquered such obstacles many times before.

CHAPTER TWELVE

OTHER BRIDGES

DURING THE YEARS of his political struggles over the bridging of the Golden Gate, Strauss's fame as a bridge builder spread throughout the country. In the late 1920's, Strauss was asked to build many bridges.

Strauss designed the bascule span of the Arlington Memorial Bridge across the Potomac, completed in 1932. That is the same bridge that was shown on television screens throughout the country thirty-one years later when the funeral procession of President Kennedy passed across its spans.

Strauss was the designer and chief engineer of the Columbia River Bridge, completed in 1932, the longest cantilever bridge in the United States. He was a consultant during the building of two great bridges between New York and New Jersey, both completed in 1931. One was the George Washington Bridge, a suspension bridge with two levels and fourteen lanes of traffic

across the Hudson River. The other was the largest steel arch
bridge in the world, the Bayonne Bridge across the Kill Van
Kull. He was co-designer of the Montreal-South Shore Bridge
in Canada, completed in 1930.

In his work on all of these bridges, Strauss was gaining valuable experience to meet his greatest challenge — the Golden
Gate. But he had long years of bridge building behind him too,
in which he had learned a thousand lessons on how to conquer
the forces of earth and sea with bridges of steel. Bridges designed by Strauss are to be found all over the country. He built
a ribbed concrete arch bridge at Belvidere, Illinois; a bridge
across the Mississippi at Quincy, Illinois; the Independence-

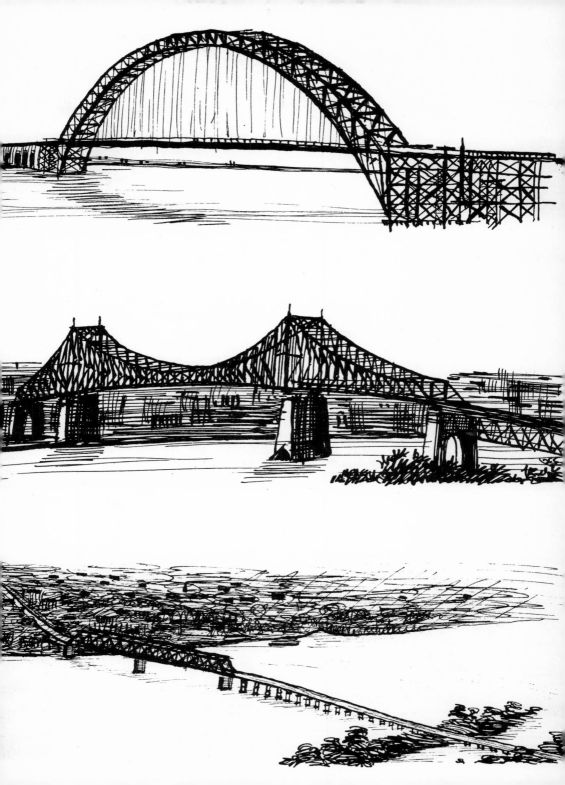

Liberty Bridge across the Missouri River; the Illinois River Bridge at Peoria, Illinois; the double-leaf bascule Burnside Bridge at Portland, Oregon; the double-leaf bascule Outer Drive Bridge in Chicago; a double-leaf bascule bridge at Sault-Ste. Marie, Michigan; a single-leaf bascúle railroad bridge across the Chicago River at 16th Street in Chicago, and another across the Calumet River in South Chicago; and many others. To this day, throughout the country, and throughout the world, cars and trains are crossing the bridges that Strauss built.

Nor were bridges his only engineering works. He invented many other things: a concrete freight car; a searchlight tower

for anti-aircraft batteries; a movable barrier to catch airplanes landing on the decks of aircraft carriers; and many other useful inventions.

With all his experience, then, Joseph Strauss, a small man, but a master of steel and concrete, stood by the Golden Gate. He was ready to build his bridge.

PART THREE

CHAPTER THIRTEEN

THE WORK BEGINS

STRAUSS DID NOT STAY with his original design for the Golden Gate Bridge. During the years of political struggle, he kept reworking his plans, like a sculptor groping for the form that he wants for a statue, cleaving away entire blocks of stone, re-shaping, changing his lines of attack.

Strauss's first plan, the bridge that was a combination of cantilever and suspension, was discarded. From his work as a consultant on the George Washington Bridge, with its sus-pended span 3,500 feet long, Strauss gained greater confidence in the suspension bridge. Now he was ready to build a single span over 4,200 feet of water — the longest span ever built.

When a man works for years on a gigantic task like the build-ing of a bridge, he is bound to grow in many ways. The change that Strauss made in abandoning the complicated combination style bridge and going to the plain suspension style bridge showed his growth as an engineer. But he was also growing in his artistic sense. Originally, he had planned to have overhead archways at each approach to the bridge. The archway on the San Francisco side was to have a gilded wrought-iron gate, and people passing through this gate would see the words GOLDEN GATE BRIDGE in great golden letters. But by the time he was ready to build his bridge, Strauss realized that these fancy archways would lessen the beauty of the bridge. Instead, he decided, he would build the bridge in stark simplicity. Its two great towers and its long graceful center span would be clear, strong artistic forms. They would have a majesty and power to match the ocean and the bay and the two jutting headlands, San Francisco and Marin, carved into a natural gateway by millions of years of tidal action.

In February of 1933 the work began. It was a great moment for Strauss, as he stood at Fort Point, his hair blowing slightly in the wind from the Pacific, and watched men and equipment moving into position. As he looked across to Lime Point on the Marin side, he thought of the sixteen long years since his first discussion with O'Shaughnessy in an office in San Francisco. Sixteen bitter years. Joe Strauss was sixty-three years old now. Already, he had spent over a quarter of his life fighting over the bridging of the Golden Gate.

He had other memories — the football field in Cincinnati, where they had used him for a football; his first bridge, for horses and wagons, built over a country stream; his months as a young engineer at the Modjeski Company; a pier built in quicksand. And now, the moment that he had been struggling for had come. He would build a web of steel across the Golden Gate that would last as long as the earth itself.

But Strauss was weakening. The terrible years of conflict had

worn him out. Maybe it was the victory that hurt him most of all. After so many years in which he had struggled to reach his goal, it was dazzling and overwhelming to suddenly be where he wanted to be. He was more used to the years of struggle than he was to the moment of victory. Now, he was like a mountain climber who has scaled a sheer cliff, never giving up, and is at the top. Looking down from the great height of his triumph, Strauss was exhausted. The nerves in his body seemed like electric wires.

Strauss went to a doctor at Stanford University. The doctor examined Strauss carefully. His diagnosis was that Strauss was in a state of collapse from nervous exhaustion.

The doctor's orders were clear and firm. Strauss would have to rest for a few months. He was not to work on the bridge until he was completely recovered. A long, peaceful sea voyage would be helpful, suggested the doctor.

On the ship that took him eastward through the Panama Canal, Strauss was often sick at heart when he thought about his bridge. I'm getting old now, he would think, and maybe I'll never have the strength to finish the job. I've practically built the bridge already — I fought to get it built, and I drew the plans for it. Someone else will have to finish it. Maybe it was too big a bridge — not too big to build, but too big for me. I haven't finished the bridge. The bridge has finished me.

But deep down, Strauss hoped that he would be back on the job, climbing on the scaffolds and watching the bridge grow, as he had done with hundreds of bridges before. To Strauss, the Golden Gate Bridge was *his* bridge — how long could he stay away from it?

For weeks, Strauss rested in the Adirondack Mountains in upstate New York. At times, he was almost able to forget the

bridge. He was almost able to think: let someone else build it. Meanwhile, he walked across small timber bridges over mountain streams, breathed in the smell of spruce and pine trees, listened to the cries of night birds, looked up at the starry skies, and spent time with his wife. As time went on, he felt relaxed. Finally, he knew that he would go back to the Golden Gate. He would finish building his bridge, so that the piers and towers and cables that he had built so often in his thoughts could be built in steel.

Back in San Francisco, the work was under way. Strauss's young assistant, Clifford Paine, was in charge. Paine had worked closely with Strauss for ten years. Strauss was not an easy man to work with. He had his own way of doing things, and could get very angry when there was a disagreement on how something should be done in the bridge-building business. His assistants usually did not stay in his company very long. But Clifford Paine was an unusual young engineer. He was not afraid to argue with Strauss and to tell him exactly how he felt. Once, Paine walked out after a quarrel with Strauss, and took another job. Suddenly Strauss realized how much he needed his brave, intelligent assistant. So he swallowed his pride and asked Paine to come back. From that time on, Strauss and Paine understood each other and worked well together.

The work on the north pier had started under Strauss's direction. Then, while Strauss was resting in the Adirondacks, Clifford Paine led the work until the north pier was finished.

In late July, 1933, with the north pier completed, Strauss arrived in San Francisco. He was ready, once more, to take command.

CHAPTER FOURTEEN

THE NORTH PIER

THE NORTH PIER, begun by Strauss and completed by Clifford Paine, was the first step in the building of the bridge. The building of the north pier was only a preview to the terrible ordeal of the building of the south pier. But even the north pier was no small task. The north pier was to be built in the water of the channel at the foot of the cliffs of Lime Point. The first step was the building of a winding road down the cliff to the channel, so that heavy equipment and materials could be moved into position.

Meanwhile, a thousand feet from the shore, the northern anchorage was being built. The anchorages of a suspension bridge are great blocks of concrete that hold the ends of the suspension cables fast. The spans of the bridge hang from the cables, but the forces that hold the entire structure up are at the points where the cables join the anchorages.

An unusual thing happened while the workers were excavating the pit where the northern anchorage would be built. They unearthed an underground spring. It turned out to be a long lost spring where the old sailing ships used to stop for water during the Gold Rush days in the 1840's. Years ago, it had suddenly disappeared. It was strange that the building of the Golden Gate Bridge, a part of the growth of modern California, should have reopened a half-forgotten past and brought back the days of the Gold Rush and early California.

The builders of the north and south anchorages reached even deeper into the past in order to get their supply of cement. In the mud flats of the southern part of San Francisco Bay, billions of oysters had left their shells over a period of many centuries. These shells had formed a material that could easily be converted into cement. A factory on the shore made cement from this oyster-shell deposit. Loads of the oyster-shell cement were carried up the bay on barges and unloaded near the anchorages. Thus, the bay and the creatures of the bay supplied the materials for the bridge at the mouth of the bay.

Other barges were being used to carry huge wooden frames from the town of Sausalito in Marin County to the channel off Lime Point. These frames were needed for the north pier construction. A cofferdam was to be built near the shore. A cofferdam is a wall used to surround a section of water. After the cofferdam is built, all of the water can be pumped out of the surrounded section. Then the concrete pier can be built inside the cofferdam. Since the north pier was to be built alongside the shore, the cofferdam needed only three sides. The cliffs of Lime Point provided the fourth side.

The wooden frames were eased off the barges and set afloat. Then they were loaded with heavy rocks so that they sank to the bottom of the channel, resting on their edges. In this way, a rough three-sided wall was built. Then, supporting walls of rock were built inside this outer barrier. Finally, the cofferdam was made as watertight as possible with a steel sheathing along its outer side. The cofferdam was complete.

The area enclosed by the cofferdam was 178 feet by 264 feet. In this area, the bridge crew dug a large excavation. For weeks, trucks poured concrete into the cofferdam, filling the excavation. After the excavation was filled, they continued to pour until the mass of concrete rose 44 feet above the surface of the water. This vast block of concrete, measuring 80 feet by 160 feet at its base (large enough to cover a large lot), and weigh-

ing ninety million pounds, was the north pier. Steel rods jutted from the top of the block. These rods would be the first part of the north tower of the bridge.

The building of the north pier was a challenging piece of engineering for the bridge builders, working as they had to do in the rushing water off the Marin shore. But the building of the south pier lay ahead, and it promised to be far more difficult.

Strauss was back on the job to lead the attack on the south pier. The south pier, which had delayed him so often in the past, because of the stories about its "plum-pudding bed rock" and its "mermaid's caverns," was ready to cause trouble again. The building of the south pier of the Golden Gate Bridge proved to be a remarkable engineering feat — perhaps the hardest single job that Strauss ever carried out.

CHAPTER FIFTEEN

THE SOUTH PIER

THE SOUTH PIER SITE was practically the open sea. The position, 1,100 feet from the shore, in a hundred feet of water, with strong tidal currents, made it a very hard place at which to build. Strauss decided that an "access trestle" was needed — a temporary wharf, which the workers could use in order to work on the south pier.

The trestle was built. Long stakes called "piles" were driven into the bedrock by explosive charges. These piles supported the trestle. The roadway of the trestle was 1,100 feet long, 22 feet wide, and was strong enough to support cranes and other pieces of machinery. Working from the end of the trestle, the bridge crew would build the south pier.

But then there was trouble. One foggy night, a big freighter crashed into the trestle and carried away 300 feet of it.

Strauss and his men rebuilt the trestle. They had hardly

completed the rebuilding when there was a storm with high winds and thunderous waves. This time, 800 feet of the trestle were swept away by the sea — and that was practically the entire trestle. There was nothing to do but build it again, once more blasting the piles into the bedrock. It seemed to Strauss that the building of the small trestle was harder than some entire bridges that he had built. Yet the trestle was only a small part of the task that lay before him.

For the south pier, Strauss decided to use a caisson instead of a cofferdam. A pneumatic caisson is a working chamber, something like an upside-down tin can, that is lowered to the bottom of the water. High air pressure keeps the water out of the caisson, so men (called sandhogs) can work inside the caisson.

In order to protect the caisson operations from the heavy seas, Strauss decided to build a huge circular wall around the south pier site. The wall would be a permanent structure that would serve as a "fender" when the bridge was completed, in order to keep ships from bumping the pier.

To build the huge fender, Strauss and his men first had to excavate a great circular pit around the pier site. Underwater explosives were used to blast this excavation in the bedrock. In this way, the builders had a fairly level, sunken area on which to build, rather than building on the sloping floor of the channel.

A guide frame was built and lowered from the access trestle. The first steel boxes of the fender were put into position by being lowered within this guide frame. Each steel box was the size of a cabin, and was merely a framework. When the first steel frame box was in position, it was filled with concrete by means of a "tremie pipe." A tremie pipe is a pipe that is used

to pour cement into an underwater construction site. The bottom end of the tremie pipe was positioned inside the steel frame, and the cement was poured through the pipe. As the level of the cement rose inside the frame, the tremie pipe was slowly raised, so that its end was always barely within the cement. Finally, the first steel frame was filled with concrete, which hardened to make it the first huge block of the fender. Then, other blocks were built next to it, and others were built on top of these. Each steel frame would be lowered by cranes, and deep-sea divers would guide it into position. Then the tremie would begin to pour, until the frame became a block of concrete.

Block by block, the great fender was built beneath the water. Finally, its walls rose above the level of the ocean. The walls surrounded a space greater than a football stadium, and full of sea water. But one break was left in the wall, at the east side. Through this open part of the wall, the caisson was towed into position and anchored on the surface of the water, inside the fender. Strauss's plan was to have the fender completed before lowering the caisson and sending the sandhogs down in the compressed air chamber to work on the pier.

Strauss lived high on a San Francisco hilltop from which he could see the Golden Gate and watch the work, when he was home. More often, he was at his Sutter Street office or at the Golden Gate, supervising the work and checking on the operations, as he did years before, when as a young engineer he built his first bascule bridge across the Cuyahoga.

On the night that the caisson was towed inside the fender ring, everything seemed to be going well. Looking down from his hilltop, Strauss could see the oval shape of the fender and the caisson at anchor within it, like a toy in the distance.

Many of the hardest problems of the task lay behind him, and Strauss was able to go to sleep with a feeling of success and accomplishment.

But at about midnight the phone rang, waking Strauss from a deep sleep. The watchman at the pier site was on the line. There was trouble. Heavy seas and gale winds were dashing the caisson about, inside the fender, hurling it against the fender walls with terrible force.

Strauss dressed hurriedly, and, after summoning several of his assistants to meet him, drove to the pier site. He stood at the end of the access trestle and looked down at the caisson. The big caisson was plunging about inside the fender like a wild animal in a cage. The heavy collisions could damage the fender walls, built with such great effort. Strauss had to make a fast decision. The caisson would have to go. The entire plan for the south pier would have to be changed.

A tugboat was summoned, and the caisson was towed out of the fender ring. Later, it was towed out to sea and sunk.

When the workmen reported for their jobs the next morning, they were surprised to find things changed. Now, Strauss ordered them to complete the fender wall. They would not use a caisson at all. Instead, the fender would be used as a coffer-dam. A tremie pipe would be used, and concrete would be poured into the underwater pier site.

The change in plans was made in October. By December, enough concrete had been poured to raise the floor of the pier site to 34 feet from the surface. Then the sea water was pumped out, and the rest of the south pier was built under dry-land conditions.

After that, all went well. The finished pier rose up to a height of 44 feet above the water. Now, with the sea defeated,

106

there was no reason to expect more trouble. Then, one foggy day, one of the workers on the pier gave a sudden shout and ran for the trestle. The prow of a big freighter had loomed up out of the fog, bearing down on the pier. But the helmsman steered the ship clear at the last moment.

At its base, the south pier was 300 feet long and 155 feet across. The hardest part of the job was complete. Now, Strauss was ready to build his towers and cables and spans. In spite of all the problems and all the criticisms, there would be a bridge across the Golden Gate. Joseph Strauss was very proud of what he and his workers had accomplished.

CHAPTER SIXTEEN

WEB OF STEEL

NEXT CAME THE TOWERS. Thousands of steel framework boxes, called cells, each about the size of a telephone booth (but about twice as tall) were riveted together, as the towers rose from the two piers. The north tower was completed long before the south tower, because the north pier was ready so much earlier.

As the towers rose, cell by cell, Strauss was there, in touch with everything that was going on. During the building of the south tower, someone asked him, "What will you do with yourself when the Golden Gate Bridge is completed?"

Strauss looked up at the riveters high above the pier, and at the growing tower. "Sometimes I think I'd like to play golf on the Lincoln Park course where I could look at the bridge," he said. Then he smiled. "But I've learned enough about building suspension bridges from this job to build one with a two-mile span. I'd like to do that. It would be the biggest bridge in the world."

However, neither golf games nor other bridges were much on Strauss's mind that spring. He still had his work of art to complete — a symphony in steel across the Golden Gate. Nothing was more important.

When the towers were finished, they rose 746 feet above the water. In each tower there were more than 5,000 steel cells. Twenty-three miles of ladders connected the cells, and Strauss had to write a twenty-six-page manual instructing the inspectors on how to find their way about within the towers. Two workmen who became lost in the north tower spent all night finding their way out again. Even Strauss himself, who had designed the towers, said "I doubt if I could find my way out of it."

Strauss gave an example of how complicated the towers were in a magazine article that he wrote at the time he was working on the bridge. He wanted to make a trip to a certain section of one of the towers. Here were the directions that he had to follow:

ROUTE 2. Enter shaft at sidewalk level and take elevator to Landing S3. Then go down ladder in Cell No. 29 to platform at elevation 486′ 4½″ and through manhole to Cell No. 28, then up ladder to elevation 491′ 11″ and through manhole to Cell No. 27, then down ladder to elevation 446′ 8½″ and through manhole to Cell No. 22, then down ladder to elevation 323′ 11″ and through manhole to Cell No. 14, and then through manhole to Cell No. 13.

With the towers built, the task which had begun with excavations in the bedrock beneath the sea now became a task in midair, as the spinning of the cables began.

Before the cables could be spun, guide lines and footbridges had to be strung over the towers, so that the workmen could work on the cables. A barge carrying a large reel of rope was towed across the Golden Gate channel by tugboats. As the barge moved across the channel, the rope was unwound, and was dropped to the bottom of the channel. But the ends of this line were kept above the water. Workmen lowered hoisting ropes from the tops of the two towers, and hoisted the line up to the tower tops. In this way, the main lines that would hold up the footbridges were strung over the towers, and their free ends were fastened at the anchorages on either shore. All ship traffic was stopped until the lines were hoisted out of the water and into position over the towers.

The footbridges were hung from these first guidelines. They looked something like the footbridges that are strung across deep ravines in wild areas of South America or Africa. However, those primitive footbridges, suspended from woven vines, are not as strong as footbridges that modern bridge builders use. The footbridges for the Golden Gate Bridge were quite sturdy and dependable, and were made mainly of redwood planking. They were kept from swaying too much by several anchoring lines which lashed them to the towers and held them steady.

The workers walked on these footbridges with complete confidence. And Joseph Strauss and the other engineers walked on the footbridges too, hundreds of feet above the sea. Men who work on bridges are not troubled by great heights; to them, the dizzy heights are part of the day's work.

But there are dangers in the building of a bridge. Joseph Strauss was determined to make the Golden Gate Bridge as safe a project as possible. Doctors and nurses were on hand to

examine the workers each day to make sure that they were in good condition for their jobs. Anyone who was slightly sick, or showed signs of dizziness, was sent home until he could recover completely. Strauss also had his men fitted with dark glasses so that they would not be temporarily blinded by the glare of the sunlight on the water.

Some bridge workers like to stunt and take chances, balancing on narrow steel girders and risking their lives unnecessarily. Strauss fired any worker who took such gambles. He was determined that lives should not be lost in the building of his bridge. He had reasons for his caution. There is an old saying among bridge men that "the bridge will have its life." Strauss knew that many lives usually were lost in the building of a large bridge. Workers and engineers have paid with their lives for the building of many great bridges. John Roebling, the great engineer who designed the Brooklyn Bridge, was killed during the construction. In the building of the Eads Bridge across the Mississippi, several of the sandhogs died as a result of the high pressure in the caisson while they were building the piers that would support the steel arches. In the building of the Quebec Bridge, eighty-two men died when the center span of the cantilever collapsed into the St. Lawrence. There had been one death early in the Golden Gate project — a worker had lost his life when a derrick failed, during the pier construction. There would be greater dangers while the men worked up high.

Strauss did something that had not been done before in the history of bridge building. He had a huge safety net strung below the footbridge, so that workers who fell might be caught, just as trapeze artists are protected by their nets. Fifteen men were saved from certain death, when they fell into the net. But

finally, there was a grim day when a heavy moving platform with twelve men on it fell into the net, carrying the net with it into the sea. Ten of the twelve men were lost. After that, there were no more deaths during the building of the Golden Gate Bridge. In spite of this terrible accident, the number of lives lost was much less than had been expected.

With the net back in place, the work of spinning the cables continued. Each of the two great cables was to be made up of more than 27,000 wires. The wires were drawn, one at a time, to stretch from the north anchorage to the south anchorage, passing over the two great towers on the way.

The wires were carried from tower to tower by reels. The reels were mounted on the guidelines. As they slid along the guidelines, the cable wire unreeled. These reels, or "traveling wheels" as they were called, traveled back and forth between the towers, controlled by the workmen with control lines. One by one, the thousands of strands of wire were strung between the towers.

The wires had to be guided over the towers and fastened at the anchorages. The tops of the towers have curved, saddle-

shaped parts known as "saddles." The wires curve over the saddles at each tower. Strong steel arms jut out from the concrete anchorages, and the ends of the wires are fastened to these. The steel arms are like gigantic fists, two at either anchorage, that hold the cables in place.

With the thousands of wires finally strung, each of the two cables was three feet in diameter. Steel clamps were fastened to the cables, and from the steel clamps hung the steel suspender bars that would attach to the span. The span was put into place in sections, as steel beams were attached to the lower ends of the suspender bars. After the span was in place, suspended from the cables, the cables were wrapped in an outer sheathing of steel wire. Joseph Strauss's web of steel had been strung across the Golden Gate.

CHAPTER SEVENTEEN

AT LAST THE MIGHTY TASK IS DONE

On May 27, 1937 the Golden Gate Bridge was opened. There were parades and fire works and ceremonies in San Francisco. At the toll plaza of the bridge, Strauss formally presented the bridge to the chief director. He was enthusiastic and proud at his moment of victory. It was a hard-fought victory — twenty years had passed since he had sat in O'Shaughnessy's office and heard the big red-faced city engineer say, in his Irish brogue, "Why don't you design a bridge for the Golden Gate? Everyone says it can't be done."

Strauss wrote a poem to celebrate the completion of the bridge. His poem starts with these lines:

At last the mighty task is done;
Resplendent in the western sun,
The bridge looms mountain high;
Its titan piers grip ocean floor,
Its great steel arms link shore with shore,
Its towers pierce the sky.

But, more than in the poem, Strauss's artistic feelings were expressed in the bridge itself. Every strand of steel, every rivet was an expression of Strauss's dream. He had designed the bridge to last "forever." Millions of people were destined to pass across the Golden Gate Bridge.

The Golden Gate Bridge is a beautiful structure, with clean, graceful lines. There are no decorations to hide the forceful steel shape. Subject to tides and winds and to possible earthquake shocks, it is an extremely strong bridge. Much of its strength is due to its flexibility. The tops of its towers can sway twenty-one feet to either side, should gales or hurricanes strike. The piers are keyed into the bedrock of the channel, giving the entire structure enormous strength.

Although the main part of the Golden Gate Bridge is a suspension bridge, with a center span of 4,200 feet and side spans of 1,126 feet each, it also has other smaller spans that lead up to it. Bridges built over flat land, in order to raise a roadway over a railroad or over other roads, are called "viaducts." On both the north and south sides, the Golden Gate Bridge starts out as a viaduct, a steel truss resting on supports that also are steel trusses. Then, just before the suspension spans begin, there are reinforced concrete pillars called "pylons" supporting the bridge. On the San Francisco side, the concrete pylons surround historic old Fort Point. The bridge over Fort Point is a steel arch, sprung between the pylons. Also, the suspended span is strengthened by a truss. So, in addition to being a suspension bridge, the Golden Gate Bridge is part truss bridge and part steel arch. The entire bridge, including the approach viaducts, is almost two miles long.

The Golden Gate Bridge has a single deck with six lanes for automobile traffic. It also has a pedestrian lane on either side, and the pedestrian toll is only ten cents, while the auto toll is twenty-five cents. The bridge is important as a part of U.S. Highway 101 that runs along the Pacific Coast from Canada to Mexico. For twenty-seven years, until the Verrazano Narrows Bridge was built in New York City between Brooklyn and Staten Island, it had the longest span in the world.

At night, the bridge is luminous with lights along its edges and beacons on its towers as a warning to aircraft. Sometimes, when thick fog drifts in from the Pacific, the bridge is completely hidden, except for its yellow lights.

The Golden Gate Bridge is a dark red color, known as "international orange." A crew of thirty painters is kept busy all year long, painting the bridge, in order to keep it in good condition, protecting it from rust and weathering.

Less than one year after the Golden Gate Bridge was completed, Joseph B. Strauss died in Los Angeles, with his wife and his sons at his bedside. But he left something behind by which he can be remembered. He left hundreds of bridges in many parts of the world. When people see the double-leaf bascule of the Arlington Memorial Bridge or the great towers of the Golden Gate, they are looking at the work of little Joe Strauss, the hundred-pound football player, engineer, poet, and artist.

Near the toll plaza of the Golden Gate Bridge, a statue of Strauss has been built. The bronze statue is green now, as happens to bronze statues when they are exposed to rain and fog. But one need only look past the bronze statue to the towers of the bridge where they jut up out of the channel to see the most important memorial to Joseph Strauss.

EPILOGUE

TIME RUSHES PAST, like the seas themselves as they move through the Golden Gate. Time does strange things — the lost bronze plate, engraved in the name of Queen Elizabeth and left by a buccaneer on a California coast, was found at the same time that Strauss and his men were building the Golden Gate Bridge. But the four centuries between Sir Francis Drake and Joseph B. Strauss are only a moment in time. In millions of years, time will do other strange things. The great mountain-building forces of the earth are still at work. In the millions of years to come, even Strauss's bridge, which he built to last forever, will have to fall.

The headlands of San Francisco and Marin may pull apart or may move closer together, in the endless upheavals of the earth. New mountains may thrust up from the floor of the channel. At last, the Golden Gate Bridge will be broken by the forces of the earth, as any man-made thing, no matter how beautiful and strong it is, must be broken.

At last, even the Golden Gate channel itself will be destroyed. All that will remain of the Golden Gate will be some small ravine in a new mountain range of the Pacific, or an insignificant strait between two small islands that used to be the peninsulas of San Francisco and Marin. Finally, even those traces will be swallowed up by the earth.

But those events lie millions of years in the future. In the meantime, the bridge stands, and is likely to stand for thousands of years. As to the past — for a time that was only a brief flicker in the history of the earth, there was a small man who dared the impossible, a builder of beautiful bridges, a man who wrestled with the giants of the earth.

INDEX

The Author

MICHAEL CHESTER received his training at the University of California at Berkeley and is now a research specialist to the missile industry. It was at Berkeley that the author took a creative writing course taught by Professor George Stewart, author of a work on the overland journey to California. This was the beginning of Mr. Chester's interest in California history and blazed the trail for his own work.

The author has written and co-written many juvenile books for Putnam, mainly on rockets and space. His latest books are *Robots in Space,* and *Let's Go to the Moon.*

Mr. Chester, his wife and three children live in Sunnyvale, California.

128